for K.

MW00964283

Overload

By

Michael Day

your friend

Michael Day

This book is a work of fiction. Places, events, and situations in this story are purely fictional. Any resemblance to actual persons, living or dead, is coincidental.

ISBN: 1-4107-0327-4 (e-book)
ISBN: 1-4107-0328-2 (Paperback)

Library of Congress Control Number: 2002096457

This book is printed on acid free paper.

Printed in the United States of America
Bloomington, IN

1stBooks - rev. 12/23/02

Acknowledgements

With heartfelt thanks to the following:
Joe Patterson,
The best personal writing coach anyone could possibly
have, and his lovely wife Pam
Helen Badder,
Whose insights breathed life into the characters in this
book
Diane Day,
The wife who walks beside me no matter what
Our six children,
Diana of Fergus, Ontario
Joe, Kelly and Jeff of Leamington
David of Charlotte, NC
Charity of Lake City, FL
Your support has made this possible.
Special thanks to Lamare Robinson for the powerful
front cover.

Table of Contents

Chapter One

The teal-colored Cadillac emerged from Belmont Circle, the new-money part of town right on schedule. Sergeant L.T. Stafford's patrol car sat waiting on Main Street. Letting the car pass he pulled out and followed.

You're going to be late again, 'Your Honor', he thought as he switched on the red lights and blew a couple of short blasts from the siren just short of Ruby's so that when the Cadillac stopped it was right in front of the diner. Lights flashing, Officer Stafford walked slowly to the driver's door.

"What the hell's this all about, L.T.?" the Mayor asked.

"License and registration, please." L.T. held out his hand.

The mayor ignored the officer's request. "I want to know just what you pulled me over for. I wasn't speeding."

"I wanted to let you know that there's a pothole in the street ahead. You might want to take it slow when you're crossing Second Avenue. Wouldn't want anything to happen to this fine automobile. I still need to see your license and registration, Randy. It's proper procedure whenever an officer stops a civilian."

"I'm not a civilian," the man sputtered. "You pulled me over to tell me about a pothole? I've about had it with your harassment. I'm the mayor of this town which means I'm your goddam boss and I resent being treated this way." He leaned his head out the window and almost shouted, "And don't call me Randy."

"Is that any way to talk to an officer of the law? I'm afraid if you don't show me your license I'll have to cite you."

"Eat shit."

The Cadillac's tires squealed as it shot from the curb, leaving L.T. standing in the street. A group of faces peered out from the large windows of Ruby's Diner, grinning and shaking their heads. He shrugged his shoulders at them and smiled.

Mayor Pruitt burst through the door of the chief's office. Conrad Mackenzie, Chief of Police, looked up at him from his desk and waved, the telephone receiver at his ear. Pruitt glared angrily and paced about the office. After a moment, Mackenzie put down the phone.

"Mr. Mayor, this is unlike you." He stood to shake the Mayor's hand. "Coming to my office, I mean. I'm usually summoned to yours."

"That man has got to go, Chief."

"Is this about Stafford again?"

"Do you listen to your police radio, Chief? Do you know that ignorant bastard pulled me over three blocks from my office, demanded my license and registration and made me sit in front of the diner with half the town looking on?"

"Were you speeding again?"

"No, goddammit." The mayor's face grew a deeper red. "Do you have any idea what that does to my image? I'm the mayor, for chrissakes. I drive the only aqua-pearl-mist Seville in White Falls. Hell, probably in Ohio for that matter. Everybody knows that's my car. And there I was sitting in it on Main Street, the busiest street in town, with a police car flashing its red lights for no reason but to get people to look at me. This is a small town, Chief. I'm sick to death of your sergeant giving people reasons to gossip about me."

The Chief sighed. "Okay, I'll call him in and talk to him again."

"Talk to him? Talk to him? No, you don't talk to him. I want him gone, off the force. Last month I'm having dinner at the Rendezvous: soft music, candlelight, fine wine, Carolyn looking radiant. What happens? The fire alarm goes off and the sprinklers drown us. Ruined her hair, her makeup, our dinner, our evening. Was there a fire? Hell no. The month before we find a family of skunks in our swimming pool. Not one skunk. A family. And they pissed in the pool the morning of our garden party. Before that my Cadillac quits on the way to the office. I had to have it towed to Griffith's. You know what he found? A potato up the tailpipe. Who arrives first to investigate in each case? Stafford. Just happened to be in the neighborhood. Bullshit. I've had it. I'm not taking any more. We're getting rid of him."

"We can't just fire him. We have no evidence whatsoever that he's connected in any way to any of your little mishaps."

"Mishaps? Little mishaps? This man hates me," the mayor said, pacing again.

"Sure holds a grudge a long time," replied the chief.

"What's that supposed to mean?"

"Well, Randy, after all, you did steal the man's wife."

"It's Mister Mayor to you, Chief. Can't I get any respect from the police in this town?" He took a chair opposite the desk. "Besides, this isn't about Carolyn." The mayor paused, then got up again. "Okay, maybe it is. But that happened ten damn years ago and the crazy sonofabitch still won't let go. We've got to do something."

"Like I said, we can't just fire him. He has thirty-one years of service. I know his record hasn't been the greatest the last few years but nowadays you need cause to let someone go."

The mayor stepped close to the desk, put his palms down on it and leaned toward the chief. "I don't want him fired," he said. "I want the bastard jailed."

"For what? We have no proof he did any of those things that happened to you."

"Come off it, Chief. We both know he's responsible. If you can't do anything, Orville will." He walked out of the chief's office leaving the door open behind him.

Orville Hennessey, father of Carolyn Pruitt and father-in-law of Mayor Randall Pruitt, owned and ran Hennessey Sand and Gravel on Route 20 just west of town. He also had a firm hand in the operation of several other White Falls businesses though few knew it save his three silent partners and a few business associates in Atlantic City. Together, they were the White Falls version of organized crime, running one sweet racket worth lots and lots of cash. The old man was rumored to be worth millions though the fact was not obvious in his lifestyle.

4

Pruitt made a left turn off Route 20 into Hennessey Sand and Gravel and was heading toward the trailer-office when he spotted Orville walking up the lane from the gravel pit shaking his head. The mayor drove past the office and on down, pulling up to talk to him.

"Morning, Orville."

"That goddam Dickie Thompson," he muttered. "Twelve years he's been working in my pits running Caterpillar front-end loaders and I still have to show him how it's done. Sonofabitch never listens until payday."

"Got time for coffee?"

"I'm ready. You're buying." He climbed in the car and they headed for town.

The breakfast crowd was gone from Ruby's Diner by the time they arrived. Pruitt was relieved to find that things had quieted. The thought of fending off questions and remarks about the latest police capture made the tiny hairs on the back of his neck stand erect. But this diner was the only place Orville would have coffee. Besides, the old man could exercise too much control in the privacy of his office.

They took a booth away from the windows and the few coffee drinkers left over from breakfast. Ruby slid two steaming cups onto the table and smiled.

"Ms. Treatt." Hennessey smiled briefly then dismissed her by looking back at the mayor. "So, what's on your mind, Randall?" Before he could answer, Hennessey spoke again. "I understand you allowed Carolyn to be made out a fool at the Rendezvous. How long are you going to let that bastard ruin my daughter's happiness?" He shook his head. "I thought we shed that no-account sonofabitch Stafford ten years ago, but you just let him go on tormenting her."

Her! What about me? thought the mayor. "That's exactly what I wanted to talk with you about." He stirred his coffee, then took a sip. "You see, I could use your help."

"Me? You're her husband; it's up to you to look after her. I handed off that responsibility years ago."

"That's not the kind of help I'm looking for." He scanned the room to see if anyone had taken notice of them. "I think we need to get rid of him."

"You're the mayor. Get the chief to fire his sorry ass and run him out of town."

"I've tried. Conrad refuses. Says he's got no proof that L.T. did any of those things. My little mishaps he calls them. He's worried about a lawsuit for termination without cause." He shrugged his shoulders. "What the hell does he care? The taxpayers will foot the bill anyway." He realized the last remark came across a little louder than he intended. Glancing around he noticed people looking in his direction so he hunched his shoulders and leaned over the table toward Orville. "Nice little diner, isn't it?" said the mayor.

"Only coffee worth drinking in these parts."

"Any idea what Ruby grosses here in a month?"

"Oh, I don't know, fifteen, twenty grand," said Hennessey. "Why? What are you getting at?"

"Try fifty. Ned says she deposits two grand or better a day."

"Better than I thought. Course, mealtimes she's pretty busy in here. Her and Priscilla run their skinny legs off."

"Isn't it about time we had a piece of that action? Twenty percent of fifty is ten grand a month. After the other partners are paid it's twenty-five hundred apiece, month after month. Would you turn down a sweet little raise in pay like that?"

"And just what the hell has all this got to do with your problem?"

The mayor grinned. "I thought you'd never ask? Do you know where Stafford lives?"

"Sure, he's got an apartment right upstairs. Ruby's his landlady."

"And that ain't all she is."

"Okay, pretty much everybody knows he's sleeping with Ruby. So what?"

"So, we go ahead and set up Ruby in the usual manner. But this time we have Conrad link Stafford to the crime. Guilt by association. Conrad tells him he either retires and gets out of town or he'll be investigated and prosecuted and will likely lose his pension over it. That leaves him no choice but to disappear forever."

The old man sat back in his seat, cocked his head a bit to one side and stared at the mayor.

The diner was closed when L.T. arrived a little after six Friday evening. He parked his Explorer in the alley behind, next to the stairs leading up to his apartment. Ruby poked her head out the back door of the diner and called out to him. When he entered she kissed him on the cheek and ushered him to a seat in the kitchen where a plate of leftover meatloaf and mashed potatoes sat steaming. Gratefully, he sat down and dug in. She filled two paper cups with coffee and pushed lids onto them.

"Take-out?" he mumbled with a mouthful of dinner.

"How about a ride?" she asked.

"Thought we usually did that in the mornings."

"Not that kind of ride. I need to pick up my car at Kendall Griffith's garage, with a quick stop by Doc Fuller's to pick up Molly."

"Everything okay?"

"Oh, sure. Just had her annual checkup, is all."

He finished up, thanked her and put the dishes in the sink. Living alone the last ten years had taught him that a little picking up could keep a kitchen, or the rest of the place, a lot more livable. Ruby followed him out the back door, carrying the coffee. When they settled into the Explorer she put L.T.'s coffee in one of the side-by-side cup holders on the lower console. The other cup holder conveniently held L.T's cell phone. Ruby sipped her coffee as they rode silently. They were comfortable together, not in love, but very much able to relax quietly together and enjoy each other's presence without having to engage in a lot of witty and stimulating conversation. That could be nice, but it made it difficult and sometimes awkward when either had something important to say.

"Tell me something, Hon," Ruby said. She knew it was his business but had to speak her mind. "How long do you think the Mayor is going to put up with your crap?"

He let out a sigh. "You're referring to that little scene in front of the diner this morning," he said. "Ruby," he paused a moment, searching for an answer.

"Randy and me go back a long way. There's a lot of bad blood between us. I swear, if he would just try something, just sucker punch me once, I'd kick the living shit out of him and be done with it."

"Done with it, is right. They'd charge you with assault, you'd be fired, probably risk losing your pension, and for what? Five minutes of knuckle busting. Look, everybody knows he married your ex-wife. But Jesus, L.T., that was ten or twelve years ago. Isn't it time to let her go?"

"This isn't about Carolyn; I just can't stand the asshole. He thinks he runs the town, the department, me. He's a first class jerk. Besides, whatever Carolyn and I had was over long before Randy blind-sided me."

"You don't like the guy so you want to punch his lights out? You're a cop; you know you can't do that just because you don't like somebody. Let it go. You know I don't like to tell you what to do. You know that. But the thing is, people are talking in the diner. They're talking about you. The whole town knows you have it in for the mayor. They know it's you that's been terrorizing him."

"Terrorizing? Shit, I'm just having fun with the smartass."

"Well, why don't you just cool it? I mean, if the town knows who's doing it, so do the mayor and the Chief of Police and those two are pretty tight. I'm just afraid you'll end up fired. Or worse."

He reached over and gave her thigh a squeeze as they pulled up in front of Doc Fuller's Animal Hospital. After a few minutes Ruby returned from the clinic. She opened the back door and her white and gray four-year-old Maltese hopped up onto the folded-down back seat and poked her head between the front buckets for L.T. to pet her. He reached around and gave her head a scratch then pulled away from the curb as Ruby settled in. They had only traveled a half-block when a large black car pulled across the street in front of them and stopped just as Molly was making her move to hop up onto the center armrest. The Explorer nose-dived under L.T.'s heavy foot, launching the chubby little dog clean over the armrest. She belly-flopped onto L.T.'s cup of coffee, which exploded in the cup holder. L.T. was cursing; his cell phone, sitting in two inches of steaming coffee, was buzzing and vibrating; the little dog was yipping somewhere under his feet; Ruby was squirming in her seat having spilled hot coffee in her lap. A man in a business suit who looked nothing like an executive sat grinning at him through the driver's window of the large black sedan. Then he was gone.

Chapter Two

Marlin Sears had stolen his first big rig at the age of 19 and still considered himself a genius for the thoughtful planning he had put into that endeavor. He had been working at the Gulf Coast Truck Salvage as a yard hand stripping usable truck parts from the wrecks. It occurred to him that a man could purchase the stripped down shell of a rig for next to nothing, transfer legal title to himself, then remove the VIN plate and attach it to a similar stolen rig in perfect condition. He'd be trucking up and down the highway in a beautiful, late-model rig without ever making a payment. After all, most of these bozo owner/operators went broke because they couldn't afford to make the payments. Marlin eliminated that problem and set himself up in business at the same time. Being without large capital investment also permitted him the luxury of choosing runs to wherever he desired since without the usual overhead he was able to undercut everyone else's freight rates. Marlin Sears was one mean businessman.

Marlin slugged another swallow from the can of Miller, slammed it on the doghouse of the Chevy van and said, "Holy shit, Carla, there it is. There's my new office."

Carla looked up from her Country Star magazine to watch the midnight blue and chrome longnose Kenworth with stainless steel refrigerated van swing a wide left into the big rig parking area of the truck stop at Wildwood, Florida.

"Shoot," said Carla, "It's just the same. It's just exactly the same as your last one. Matter of fact, it's just the same as mine."

"It's newer."

"Oh my god, I best rush home and write that in my diary. Dear diary: we just risked our lives to steal another nothing-blue truck. Christ, Fish. For once let's get a red one." She pointed toward a red Peterbilt parked in the front row of rigs along the east side of the restaurant. "Yonder's a real pretty truck. I want that one. Or what about that bright yellow, banana-looking tractor over there. Man, there's even a purple one. But no, we have to have another nothing-blue truck." She threw the magazine on the floor and crossed her arms.

"Are you wound too tight, sister? You know how I feel about bright-colored trucks. You steal one of them you're just begging to get caught." He swung in the seat, facing her now and waved a finger. "Never stand out in a crowd. If you stand out people remember you, can give a description. Next thing you know, the Sheriff's at your door. I run a successful trucking business because I keep a low profile and I stick to my guns."

Carla spat out the window of the van. "Well, I know that in your mind you're a legend in the corporate world. But somehow, I don't call two stolen eighteen-wheelers a successful conglomerate." She spat again because she knew it pissed him off.

"Hush your mouth, girl, he's heading for the back row. If he walks out carrying his travel bag that means we go to work."

Marlin taught Carla how to handle a rig, too. There were times he wished he hadn't. She always thought she was the better driver, which meant he constantly had to demonstrate the opposite.

Marlin prided himself in knowing what to look for when he wanted a new rig. When this blue KW pulled in the first thing he checked was the exhaust pipe on the trailer's diesel-powered refrigeration unit. It was not smoking, which meant the trailer likely wasn't loaded, at least, not with perishable goods. When the trailer's wheels bounced over a pothole in the parking lot it confirmed his expectations that the trailer was empty and the driver was likely going to spend some time inside the truckstop, have a shower, have dinner, wait for a load.

It is easy to snatch a tractor out from under an empty trailer. The landing gear goes down easily with the hand crank; the fifth wheel pin pops nicely. He'd drive right out from under it, exit the driveway to the west of the restaurant and be halfway to Zephyrhills before that driver stepped out of the shower.

Marlin started the van and drove it slowly out of the parking lot onto SR44 then doubled back on the west side of the restaurant where the building was without windows. They inched ahead without lights. Carla leaned forward in the passenger seat as they reentered the truckstop from the rear of the restaurant. She spotted the shining, stainless steel trailer as it made it to the back row of the parking area, the most remote section of the lot.

"Shit," said Marlin. "I bet he's looking for a lot lizard. That's the only reason he'd park this far out. He's after pussy. We could be here all night while he hangs around his CB radio trying to find a beaver to get his rocks off. Let's get out of here."

"Wait," said Carla. "Let him park it. If he is looking for a hooker and he's got six bits worth of self-respect he'll go inside for a shower first. That'll give us plenty of time to snatch it. Hell, I wouldn't want no stinking, sweating truck driver jumping my bones. I like them smelling pretty when they saddle me up."

His backhand caught the left side of her lips. She touched a finger to the trickle of blood at the corner of her mouth, examined it and smiled. "God, I love it when you're rough," she teased. "Don't worry, big brother. I'll save you some."

He was about to strike her again, wipe the grin off her face when she nodded, looking forward out the window and whispered, "There he is."

Arnold Perkins had a sweet deal. The 55-year-old second-generation farmer spent summers tilling the family farm in upstate New York. He endured winters supplementing his farm income by filling in for a handful of independent trucker friends who needed a week or two away from the grind without sacrificing business to do it. Arnold only took Florida runs; he wanted no part of any longer trips and wasn't going any place that wasn't warm. With him as a temporary driver an owner/operator could enjoy a much-needed vacation with family while Arnold would truck away to the Sunshine State to give his arthritic joints a respite from the bitter cold of the North and when the urge hit him, to sew a few wild oats with a young truckstop cutie, for a few bucks, of course.

This particular run was unusual because it occurred in September nearing harvest time. He wouldn't ordinarily leave his corn crop this time of year but a neighbor whose pregnant young wife was about to calf wanted to be close to home when the event took place. He couldn't afford to shut his truck down so Arnold finally agreed to take just one run to Florida. He figured the corn was okay for three weeks or so yet and his equipment was in pretty good shape and wouldn't require a lot of prep time for harvest. Besides, he had had a hankering lately for a little strange poontang so what the hell.

Florida summers stretched through September. Even with air conditioning it proved a bit much for Perkins and he was glad to shut the rig down at Wildwood, have a night off. He looked forward to a shower now almost as much as he did after a fourteen-hour day of farming caked the loam about his leather neck. After the water ritual, he would eat a meal then return to the truck and wait for the college girls to come down from Gainesville to earn their tuition. They were like children at an Easter egg hunt, wandering the parking lot in search of drivers who would pay for a little personal service. In the morning he'd be in Brooksville loading grapefruit for the trip home. Clutching his travel bag in his right hand he strolled toward the truckstop.

Marlin slipped the van between two rigs and switched off the engine. He took the Slim Jim from the tool kit between the seats. "All right," he said to Carla and sucked in a breath of steamy, evening air. "Follow the plan." They got out of the van without another word, Marlin to steal the truck; his sister to make sure its owner was occupied.

Carla cut between two trailers to catch up to the trucker. She would fall in behind him and tail him to the truckstop entrance. As she slipped past a blue and orange Roadway Transport tractor unit a man leaned out the driver's window and whistled.

"Hey Foxy, up here. Bring that sweet ass up here. I got the money if you got the time."

Carla wheeled around to face him, startled by the driver's voice. "Fuck you, asshole. I'm a driver. Why don't you jerk yourself off to Miami, look for a lot lizard there." She spat and moved on. The driver called after her but didn't follow. Her eyes scanned the driveway between the rows of trucks but couldn't spot Arnold Perkins. She ran between two trucks in the next row and stopped ahead of them to look for the guy with the travel bag but still there was no one. She cursed under her breath.

Marlin stood on the fuel tank step on the driver's side of the blue Kenworth. He steadied himself by gripping a mirror bracket with one hand while his other hand gently eased the Slim Jim upward. The lock yielded with a familiar click that brought a smile of pride to his lips. He spent a moment too long admiring his work.

"Just what in hell do you think you're doing, redneck?"

Marlin froze at the sound of the man's voice. He turned to look at the driver's face but instead his gaze caught the glint of light from a nickel-plated revolver, the barrel of which pointed directly at his chest and kept him from offering any reply at all. For a moment the only sound came from truck tires whining on I-75 a few hundred yards away.

This was not part of the plan. It was Carla's responsibility to tail this guy and create a diversion if he posed any kind of threat to the operation. Failing that, she was supposed to warn him of impending danger so that he would never find himself staring death or capture in the face. Where the hell was she? If he survived this his sister would find herself in shit nearly as deep.

The subtle click of the gun's hammer cut the stillness as Arnold cocked the weapon, making ready to protect his neighbor's property by blasting this thief to hell. Marlin couldn't move a muscle. He had never faced a firearm but had witnessed the deadly force they carried. His stare remained fixed on the barrel when, suddenly, it tipped downward toward the pavement and went off with a flash of fire and an ear-splitting bang. Marlin hit the ground and crouched there a moment. Arm still outstretched, the gun now loose in his hand, Arnold Perkins' eyes widened, head lowered. His jaw dropped, as did Marlin's when he spied the bloody tip of a number seven Crafters screwdriver protruding from the driver's shirt, shreds of flesh from his heart and lung clinging to it and looking blackish under the orange lot lights. A slender hand reached around, plucked the smoking revolver from him and he went down like a sack of grapefruit. Arnold Perkins would never again amuse himself with poontang, strange or otherwise.

Marlin patted himself all over, looking for blood. Surprisingly, he felt no pain. He thought being shot must hurt but he felt nothing. Must be the adrenaline, he thought. He picked himself up from the pavement and moved from behind the truck to an area under a nearby light where he examined himself. Nothing. "He missed me," he said, chuckling to himself.

Carla Sears stood quivering, her body alive from the tremendous surge of adrenaline that had set every nerve on fire with energy needed for her soft, silky hands to ram the business end of a screwdriver clean through the chest of a full grown man without any difficulty at all. Her mouth gaped, then slowly curled into a grin.

"Did you see that?" she gasped. "Did you see that sonofabitch go down?" She was shaking, and grinning.

Marlin stepped down from the truck. "Jesus, Carla, what are we going to do now? I can't believe you killed this guy." Marlin was trembling too, uncontrollably as the adrenaline surged through him supercharging his nervous system.

"Let's get the hell out of here before somebody sees us. That shot had to be heard a mile away. My goddam ears are ringing."

"What about him?"

"Leave him. Let's go."

"Are you spun, woman?" The glow of lights from an approaching rig began to light up the parking lot in front of the truck. "Shit, here comes somebody now. Let's get him out of sight." He grabbed the wrist of the blood-soaked driver and dragged his remains as quickly as he could toward the rear of the truck's trailer. Carla slipped the gun barrel inside the waist of her jeans and hurried to take the dead man's other wrist. One of Perkins' shoes slipped off and bounced into the weeds beyond the edge of the asphalt as they swung him around behind the trailer. They let go of his arms and his head hit the pavement with the sound of an overripe watermelon just as a tractor-trailer idled past the front of Perkins' truck.

"Okay," said Carla. "Now let's get our asses out of here."

"We can't just leave this slob here. The cops-."

"The cops? The cops can't do shit, Fish. How they gonna know who killed some dumb Yankee trucker in the back of a truck stop?"

He waved a finger at her. "Carla, they have all kinds of scientific shit to find killers nowadays. DNA and stuff. They come in here and suck up everything in vacuum cleaners, they find a nose hair, run it through their computers and find out it's got your name on it. You pull into a scale house one day, you're thinking you got the world by the ass and bam, you're surrounded by State Troopers, FBI, whoever else wants to be on the eleven o'clock news. Three weeks later you're found guilty and sentenced to die by lethal injection."

He grabbed the lever on one of the trailer's barn doors, lifted it out of its rest and swung it, pulling the door open. Carla automatically did the same with the other door. "Come on," he said, "Let's put him in the reefer." He slipped his hands under the dead man's shoulders and lifted. Carla wrapped her fingers around the lifeless ankles and heaved upward.

"Christ, this guy must weigh two hundred pounds." Heaving the body up, it banged against the trailer's steel bumper assembly. They struggled to hold the corpse at waist height long enough to get a better grip.

Marlin maneuvered his hands under Perkins' back and pushed upward and into the trailer. The body flopped over like a mackerel and lay face down on the ribbed aluminum floor. Without thinking Marlin rubbed his palms on the thighs of his jeans to wipe off the blood.

"You stupid ass." Carla spat. "You're the one talking DNA and you just rubbed it all over yourself. You deserve to get caught."

Marlin stared at the bloody smudges on his jeans. He threw up his hands. "I'll get rid of the jeans when we get back to the ranch." He closed and latched the trailer doors. "Get the glad hands," he said. "I'll raise the landing gear. Don't forget to latch the fifth-wheel pin."

"You're taking the trailer? With the dead guy?" She couldn't believe he would do such a thing. She had almost begged him for a stainless steel Great Dane. No way would he budge. Too flashy. Stands out. People remember you. Asking to get caught. Now, here was a fifty-three foot gem complete with twenty-four inch polished aluminum wheels and radial Michelins and he was actually going to haul it away with a corpse inside dripping fresh blood all over the bumper.

"We can't leave it here. Our fingerprints are on it, DNA, all that scientific shit. If we haul it out of here maybe nobody will know he was ever here. He never made it inside. Maybe nobody will look for him for a week or so. If the whole rig is gone his outfit will figure he's gypsying for some other company. We've got to get it out of here." Carla shook her head but headed for the cab of the tractor, climbed onto the catwalk and began coupling the airlines to the trailer. Marlin wound the crank on the trailer's landing gear and the Kenworth squatted just a bit as the trailer settled back down onto it. He climbed back up onto the step and slid the Slim Jim out of the door. Then he hopped to the front of the rig and swung open the fiberglass hood and fenders. In a few seconds more he had run a hot jumper to the fuel solenoid and crossed the starter contacts with a screwdriver. The truck shuddered as the Caterpillar diesel rumbled to life then settled into a gentle idle.

"What are you doing, Fish?" She was scolding him now.

"I'm starting the goddam truck. What the hell you think I'm doing?"

"Did you ever stop to think that maybe these would be quicker?" She waved the keys she had fished from Perkins' pocket. She knew she had him now. She had saved his ass and she knew she had it over him. "This rig is mine, shiny trailer and all. You drive the van home."

"Bullshit. We're not partners, Carla. We're not keeping this trailer, we're just taking it long enough to get rid of this driver then we'll burn it or ditch it somewhere nobody will find it. Down in the Glades. I'm in charge of this company; I make the decisions."

"You weren't in charge of jack shit when you were looking up the barrel of that dude's iron. If I hadn't saved your ass you'd be dead as him right now." She jumped down from the catwalk and opened the cab door. Fishing a rag from behind the driver's seat, she threw it at him. "Go and clean the blood off the back of my new trailer."

He walked over to her, pulled the gun from her britches and stuffed it down the back of his jeans then

took the rag and stomped off toward the rear of the rig.
"We'll settle this at the ranch, bitch."

Chapter Three

Carla could be such a bitch sometimes. Marlin couldn't believe he had let her walk all over him. She was not going to be a partner and she was not going to keep the stainless steel Great Dane Trailer or his new Kenworth tractor, he would see to that when they got things cleaned up at the ranch. He followed the stolen rig out of the truckstop, keeping the van a safe distance behind. The plan was to make a right turn out of the parking lot onto State Road 44 west, follow it for eighteen miles to Inverness where they would catch US 41 south for twenty-one miles. A left at US 98 just outside of Brooksville would cut back across Interstate 75 and take them twelve miles east to Route 301 south which would run them through Dade City to the ranch just outside of Zephyrhills. It was long and convoluted but it would keep them off the Interstate where there was always the chance of some driver from this guy's outfit recognizing the rig. The last thing Marlin wanted now was another confrontation with an ugly Yankee.

The only flaw in the plan was that his sister chose not to follow it. Instead of turning right she swung the rig left onto State Road 44 and immediately right, onto the southbound ramp to I-75. He grabbed the microphone on the CB and keyed it, paying no attention to the two drivers already chattering incessantly. "What the hell is this?" Because of his proximity, his radio signal was strong enough to totally obliterate the ongoing conversation.

"Shut up, Fish," Carla replied.

They had agreed there would be none of the usual CB conversation until the rig was back at the ranch and "cleaned", meaning all identifying marks, tags and VIN plates had been changed. The rig picked up speed quickly with its trailer empty. Carla shifted smoothly through thirteen forward speeds. Marlin was steaming along behind her, edging ever closer to the rear of the Great Dane and his boiling point.

"Don't you hush me, woman." He was pissed but had sense enough not to call her by name. "I'm still the boss. Back her down."

She was flying now, booting through seventy, seventy-five. "Oh, you're the boss?" She laughed into the microphone. "Boss this." She switched off the radio, kicked the loafer off her left foot and raised it to rest on the dash. Leaning back in the Bostrom air-ride seat, her hands at four and eight o'clock on the oversize steering wheel, she liked the way her new rig cruised.

"Slow down," shouted Marlin. "Slow down, dammit." He threw the mike at the dash.

Carla bounced along, the air-ride seat a little too lively, obviously set for the weight of a large man. She reached down with her left hand and tugged the valve to let out some air and soften the ride. Even empty, she liked the way the new rig handled. With the flip of a switch the interior lights came on. In quick glances, her instinct never allowing her eyes to be off the road for long, she took a look around the cab.

She switched the CB radio back on and listened for a moment to two drivers cackling back and forth in the distance. Her thumb squeezed the microphone button and she spoke.

24

"Hey, Fish. I take back what I said about this one being just the same as yours. This ain't a sleeper, it's a driver's lounge. Shoot, it's got a fridge, closet, TV/VCR combo and would you believe a dinette. This here's one of them big trucks."

"Slow down, Spider." He tried to say it without clenched teeth but his anger came through loud and clear. "Just slow it down, would you?"

"It's got two bunks too," she went on, ignoring him. "I swear, it's like a two-story condominium. Oh, I can see me having some all night bloomer-shucking parties in this rolling rumpus room."

She was about to tell him more when another voice cut in.

"Who is that sweet young thing in that big truck?" a driver crooned.

"It's Spider Woman," Carla called back.

"Did you say Spider Woman? Spider? Like in Black Widow?"

"Yeah, that's me. Black Widow, I like that. Yeah. Just call me Black Widow, I'm a real man killer."

"Which way you going, Black Widow?"

"I'm southbound and heading for the house."

"Damn, if I ain't always a day late, a dollar short and heading in the wrong direction. You be careful rolling south, Black Widow there's a full-grown bear sitting in the median near the Brooksville cutoff and he's shooting the southbound side. Have a safe one. I'm the Handyman, northbound movin' on."

"Thanks, Handyman. Guess I better back it down. You're looking good to Wildwood, that's where I got on."

Carla eased back on the accelerator and let the rig settle down to sixty miles per hour. Marlin had been following so closely in the van that he nearly collided with the slowing trailer. Carla chuckled as she looked in the mirror and saw the van swerve wildly into the left lane. When she glanced ahead again she spotted the sign for a rest area. It meant they were getting close to U.S. Highway 98, the Brooksville cutoff. She switched on the truck's right turn signal in preparation for taking the ramp into the rest area.

"What do you think you're doing?" Marlin's voice came over the CB speaker.

"Got to water my lily," Carla replied.

"Christ, we'll be home in twenty minutes."

"Maybe not," she said into the microphone. "I think I should drop off my passenger first." The radio went silent.

Marlin followed the rig into the rest area and parked beside it in one of the angled, truck parking spaces. He was standing next to the driver's door looking up at the window as Carla climbed down from the shiny, blue Kenworth. She jumped from the tank step, detoured around Marlin and headed for the rest room. It was nearly midnight and the parking lot was two-thirds full of trucks.

He called after her. "Just what are you intending to do with him?"

"Dump him," she called over her shoulder, still walking briskly.

He ran to catch up and grabbed her arm, turning her around. "We need to bury him." His voice was hushed now. "We can't just dump him anywhere. He'll be found."

"So what?"

"Jesus, Carla," he shook his head. "Your clutch is slipping. If nobody finds him, he's just another dude gone missing, they figure likely he ran off and they forget about him. But they find him dead and it's murder, no question about it. They don't forget about murder. They hunt you down like a wounded deer."

"Let me remind you of something, Fish. This guy is dead because your ass needed saving and I'm the one who saved it. And if I hadn't, you'd be just as dead as he is. Now, all we have to do is dump him in the river and he's gator bait. By sunup there's nothing left to find. You really want to shovel all night, then be forever shit-scared someone's going to dig him up?"

He let go her arm, stared at her a moment, turned and walked back to the van.

Carla barely had the rig back to cruising speed when she came upon the State Trooper she had heard about. The patrol car was parked in the median facing north with radar aimed at the southbound lanes. It was just opposite the sign for U.S. 98, the Brooksville cutoff, as it was most commonly known. But 98 was also the most direct route to Dade City and, by extending down U. S. 301 from Dade, to Zephyrhills. As long as the cop was sitting on the Interstate there would likely be no one to interfere with their disposal of the body. She slowed and took the ramp, then turned left onto U.S. 98 south. Less than a mile from I-75 she coasted the rig to a stop halfway across the Withlacoochee Bridge, the truck hugging the rail. Carla switched off all lights, set the parking brakes and left the engine idling. No lights were visible in either direction as she climbed down from the Kenworth. Only the clatter of the idling diesel broke the stillness of the Central Florida night. A misty fog rose from the black waters of the Withlacoochee River and the humidity was choking.

By the time she reached the rear of the trailer, Marlin had both of its barn doors open. Carla took the ankles, Marlin the shoulders and they· heaved. The body slid easily on the ribbed aluminum floor of the trailer but once it cleared the doors the weight was too much for Carla and she lost her grip on the dead man's legs. Marlin stumbled under the additional weight and fell against the bridge railing. Without a word they each grabbed an arm and stood the stiffening man upright against the rail then leaned his head and shoulders over it. They moved to his legs and hoisted upward and Arnold Perkins' final exit was an awkward swan dive, splashing loudly into the Withlacoochee River whose waters run so murky they are black night or day.

At the center of Zephyrhills Carla wheeled the rig through a left turn onto SR54 and headed east out of town. A mile and a half past the city limits she swung a wide right into what looked like a vacant lot with a driveway down the middle. The truck's lights disappeared under a cluster of spreading, moss-hung live oaks. After a couple hundred yards the rig emerged as the grove ended and the house and barn came into view in the headlamps. Carla maneuvered the huge transport past the house and through the barn's open doors. She shut off the engine, jumped down and headed for the house, dragging the barn door closed behind her.

The ranch wasn't much but it was the only home they had ever known. It was hardly more than a shack: a two-bedroom, clapboard sided, tin-roofed frame house with porches and screen doors front and rear. It had no central heat or air conditioning, just a fireplace in the living room to warm the winter nights and nothing at all to spell the searing humid days and nights of summer, and in Central Florida that's all there is: summer and winter with almost no spring and fall to buffer.

This was the place where Arlo Sears had come to cure his gambling addiction, not the worst of his vices. On a hundred and thirty-five acres of scrub pasture with a stream cutting it diagonally, Sears tried to raise beef cattle. During that time, Marlin was born in March of 1970, Carla eleven months later. Before he could knock up his battered wife a third time she ran off with a migrant farm worker from South Texas, leaving her infant children with no mother and no lasting memory of one. Arlo managed to hang onto the ranch, raised a small herd of beef, enough to survive on and to subject his children to untold misery, indignation and terror throughout a lifetime of abuse which included mental, physical and sexual horrors, none of which was ever known outside the ranch.

You couldn't see the place from the road. It lay completely hidden behind the grove of live oaks and that was all right with the folks of Zephyrhills. Once the children were old enough Arlo would send them to town for any supplies or groceries necessary. The elder Sears was almost never seen in town, although he'd been known to escort his youngsters a time or two to the Salvation Army Thrift Store to clothe them. He tried to put on the appearance of a gentleman but folks could tell he wasn't kind to his offspring.

Arlo's only other excursions were trips to Tampa that would last three or four days at a time. He would always come home drunk and blabbering about a card game or a dice game that had him close to a fortune. But he never came home with money and that made him even meaner.

When Marlin was just sixteen, he told Everett Flood, his boss at the truck wrecking yard, that his old man had run off and never came back. Just disappeared, or so the story went. No one ever looked for him because he was never actually reported missing. Arlo Sears was pretty much forgotten by everyone but his two children, who knew exactly what had become of him and wanted most of all to be able to leave his memory behind.

Marlin was leaning against the counter, sucking back a Budweiser when Carla entered the kitchen. She pulled one from the refrigerator, popped the top and swished a mouthful of the cold beer, swallowing hard. She sat at the table and started pulling off her work boots and shaking her head.

"Man, did you see that sonofabitch go down?"

"You're fucking spun, you know that?" He glared at her but she was still grinning. "Seventy-five miles an hour in a truck with New York tags and a corpse in the trailer. That's not just stupid, Carla. That's stupid and fucking crazy. Your brain's on overload."

"Overload? Overload? You weren't talking about overload when I saved your sorry ass. Don't talk to me about overload because you wouldn't be here if I hadn't saved the day, Fish."

He slammed the beer on the counter, his nostrils flared. "You just don't get it, do you, Carla? We killed this guy tonight. That's murder, Carla. That's the death penalty and you're playing games."

He was standing over her now, shaking with anger. She stood up and faced him.

"Relax. We're not going to get caught."

"Relax? Christ, Carla. You don't follow the route we agreed on and you drive like you're asking the FHP to chase you. It was like you were trying to get caught."

"I knew what I was doing. I backed it down when we got close to the cop. I was just having fun with you."

Marlin slapped her. She went over backwards, the chair slamming the floorboards. Her lip was bleeding again.

"Don't fuck with me, Carla."

She got to her feet and faced him again. Her fingers touched the trickle of blood on her cheek. A smile came to her lips, then she slapped him back. He grabbed a handful of her hair and pulled. She clutched at his crotch and squeezed. He tugged at her hair, jerking her head back. She began to massage him through his jeans. He pushed her down to her knees and she went for his belt buckle. He forced her face into his groin, but instead of fighting she took him into her mouth and gripped his buttocks for leverage. He thrust hard into her face a few times, charged with sexual energy. But with every move he made, Carla countered with one of her own and he came to realize that the more he tried to inflict pain, the more pleasure she took from him. She was in the driver's seat and that was not what he wanted.

He stood her up roughly and tore her shirt off. He clawed at her jeans, tugged them to her ankles, pushed her back on the table and drove into her with a powerful thrust. She dug her fingers into his back and moaned. No matter how roughly he treated her, she reacted as though she felt true bliss and he knew she had beaten him. She had killed to save him and she would never let him live it down. She was forcing him to surrender to her. Never again would he control her. Never again would he be the boss. From now on she was a full partner, in the business and everything else.

Saturday morning there was no mention of the previous night's confrontation in the kitchen. There never was. Carla rose late. It was after ten when she poured a cup of coffee from the already half-gone pot and headed outside. Marlin was in the barn and had already switched the tags and VIN plate and was using a buffing wheel with rubbing compound to erase the name of NY Truck Brokers from the door of the Kenworth.

"Get a bucket and brush," he called to her. "Scrub the blood out of the trailer." He pointed to a green plastic garbage bag. "Gather up whatever clothes you had on last night. We'll burn them with the rest of his things."

Ignoring him, Carla walked around to the passenger door and climbed inside with her coffee. She stepped into the spacious sleeper compartment and admired its luxurious appointments. After a moment she began rifling through drawers and compartments, removing any personal items and dropping them in a heap on the truck's floor.

The low rumble of a motorcycle engine became suddenly audible as an old yellow Harley-Davidson emerged from the cover of the live oaks and idled roughly up the sandy driveway. Carla followed her brother out the barn door. A black man in a yellow Hawaiian shirt, red leather skull cap and goggles stopped the motorcycle near the house and sat astride it, staring at them and the shiny rear doors of the trailer visible in the barn. Instinctively Marlin reached for the handle of the barn door and slid it shut.

"Something we can help you with?" he called out to the stranger.

"Sorry to trouble you folks," he said. "My hog's running a bit rough this morning. Would y'all have a screwdriver I could borrow?"

Marlin fished a Crafters from his hip pocket, walked over and handed it to the man. "How'd you find this place?" he asked.

The stranger leaned over and adjusted the mixture screw on the bike's carburetor. The rumbling engine smoothed a bit.

"Just took the first driveway when she started acting up. Didn't know what I'd find here."

"Seems to be okay now," Carla called out. "Maybe you should move on."

The stranger smiled and handed back the screwdriver. He thanked them before turning the old bike around and disappearing under the trees, sand and smoke spitting from the Shovelhead Harley.

By noon the sanitation of the new rig was complete. There was no visible trace of its previous operation under NY Truck Brokers. Now the door decals read "Sears Refrigerated Transport Service." Marlin was admiring his work when Carla called from the house that lunch was ready.

She had fried slabs of ham and served it with boiled okra and cold pinto beans. Marlin poured himself a cup of coffee and sat down.

"What's the schedule this week?" Carla asked.

He pointed to the clipboard next to the phone. "We both load Monday morning. You pick up grapefruit in Vero Beach and haul ass to Cleveland, Ohio. I'm loading celery out of Belle Glade to Bumfuck, Wisconsin."

Chapter Four

L. T. Stafford always got his best sleep in the wee hours of the morning, if he slept at all. Sleep had never been a problem in his younger years. But as he inched upward toward fifty he seemed to grow more and more subject to long, lonely nights of self-examination that medically would be labeled insomnia. Now, at fifty-three, he could count on not sleeping at all at least two or three nights a week. Some nights were not a total washout. When he finally crashed it would be in the abbreviated hours just before dawn. It was then that sleep slammed him like a hammer and he would be purely comatose for at least a couple of hours, maybe more.

For that reason, and maybe one or two others, Ruby Treatt had volunteered to help him wake up in the mornings to ensure he didn't miss a shift and give the White Falls Police Department further reason to fire him. Ruby would toss her apron on the counter at about six-fifteen and slip out the back door of Ruby's Diner, leaving Priscilla to run things for a few minutes.

This particular morning was no different. She tiptoed up the back stairs to his porch, fished inside the bird feeder for the key, and let herself in. His snoring was audible over the rattle and hum of the window air conditioner. A holstered, police-issued pistol hung from the bedpost. She walked over and stood beside the bed and looked at his bare back sticking out from under the white cotton sheet, pulled the banana-clip from her hair and set it silently on the night table. Her fingers tugged at the zipper of her uniform. The frock fell in a heap at her feet, the rest of her clothing soon followed. She slipped under the sheet and felt his cool skin against her breasts and tummy. Her hand reached around to brush at the hair on his stomach then stroked downward. His rhythmic breathing quieted suddenly.

He raised one eyelid to squint at the digital clock on the dresser. "You're early," he grunted.

"Good morning to you too," she whispered, her lips brushing his left ear. Is that extra heat you're packing or are you just glad to see me?" She tried to stroke him but he clamped a massive hand about her wrist.

"Excuse me," he said. "But I need to go."

"Go later. I don't care if it is piss-hard. Let's not waste that masterpiece."

L. T. rubbed his eyes a moment, considering her offer. He let go of her wrist. "Didn't we just do it yesterday?"

"Couldn't have," she said, "I would have remembered." She stroked him.

"No," he thought aloud, "No, I distinctly recall busting you yesterday morning for possession of crack." He relaxed a moment and allowed himself to enjoy her caresses then reached a hand behind him to clutch her left buttock.

Ruby leaned back and said, "Are you sure that was me, L. T.? I mean, I'll bet in your line of work you must encounter numerous beautiful young women that you can threaten with arrest just to get them naked."

He smiled at her teasing. "Ruby, I'd know your sweet ass anywhere. But then, who in White Falls wouldn't?"

Ruby released her grip on his erection, yanked the pillow from beneath his head and pushed it down over his face. She climbed atop him and squealed, "Don't you say that about me, L. T. For your information I'm very selective about who I sleep with."

"Selective is right," he chuckled, his voice muffled by the pillow. "You're always selecting somebody."

Ruby pounded the pillow with her fists. "I don't see no halo over your head," she cried. "Besides, it's no crime to enjoy a little horizontal bop from time to time you know. How'd you like it if I just let your sorry ass sleep? The chief could have his way and fire your tail right off the force. Wouldn't that make Mr. Mayor Pruitt the cock of the walk in this town-."

He took the pillow from her, pulled her down and locked his lips to hers. She struggled at first, acting as if her feelings had truly been hurt, then gradually yielded in the certainty of having her way with him after all. As they kissed, Ruby snuggled her naked body closer to his. Then the phone rang.

The voice of Conrad Mackenzie, Chief of Police, chased the smile from his lips. "My office, oh-eight-thirty sharp. Mayor Pruitt will also attend." The line went dead. He held the phone above its cradle, considering the significance of the Chief's message.

"Duty calls?" Ruby asked.

He put down the phone and swung to face her on the bed. "Maybe for the last time." L. T. rose from the bed and headed for the bathroom. Ruby dressed silently and slipped out the back door.

There were two people that Sergeant L. T. Stafford would least like to face at eight-thirty on a Monday morning or pretty much any other time. One was his ex-wife Carolyn who had tolerated him some twenty-two years. The other was the man she left him for: Mr. Mayor Randall Pruitt, the self-proclaimed most intelligent individual in all of Sandusky County. This meeting was almost certain to be another retirement counseling session in which the mayor and the chief would apply more pressure upon him to leave the force. Thirty-three years of enforcing the law, fighting crime and protecting the citizens of White Falls and instead of saying thank you they just wanted him gone. He entered the Chief's office without knocking and was caught off guard by the sight of Ned Dunphy, the general manager of the White Falls Savings and Loan, seated opposite the desk of Chief Mackenzie. Mayor Pruitt was yet to arrive and L. T. hoped he had begged off this meeting. Dunphy and the chief turned to glare at him.

"Oops," said L. T. starting to back out. He had fully intended to interrupt the mayor and for a moment was genuinely embarrassed to see that the attempt had backfired. Then he realized it was Dunphy he had barged in on and he relished that nearly as much.

Chief Mackenzie waved him in and said, "L. T., you know Mr. Dunphy of the White Falls Savings and Loan."

Dunphy rose and extended a hand. "Dumpy," L.T. nodded at the banker as he sat down. "Where's Randy?" he asked the chief.

Chief Mackenzie looked up from the document he had been studying on his desk. "His Honor Mayor Pruitt extends regrets that he will be late in arriving but is still planning to attend this meeting," he said, his formality as much a signal to L. T. to be businesslike as it was an acknowledgment of Dunphy's stature as a local businessman.

But L. T. could not resist the opportunity. "Honor?" He was too old and too close to the door to be influenced by the Chief's demeanor. And he still held a grudge against Ned Dunphy that would not permit his ego to offer respect to that particular small-town nobleman either. Ten years ago when L. T. and Carolyn were engaged in liquidating and dividing their community property and L. T. found himself in a short-term cash squeeze, Dunphy had refused him a line of credit citing low cash reserves at the S&L. L. T. was confident that that was a lie concocted as a result of pressure by Dunphy's friend Randall Pruitt to try to force him into personal bankruptcy and further humiliation. L. T. was not likely to forget Dunphy's role in his struggle to keep the bills paid and maintain credibility.

But he couldn't figure out why Dunphy was attending a meeting of any kind at Police Headquarters, especially a meeting with the chief and the mayor. It couldn't be a retirement counseling session as he had surmised.

"So, what's up, Connie? What's Dumpy doing here? Is he offering bankruptcy planning for police retirees?"

Chief Mackenzie almost ignored his sarcasm, except to scowl at his sergeant. "Mr. Dunphy has a duty to this community to notify the authorities whenever he encounters suspected unlawful activity. He is here today with evidence that may indicate that a certain individual in White Falls is engaged in money laundering activities."

Mister Mayor Randall Pruitt entered the room without knocking. Ned Dunphy rose to shake his hand. L. T. and the chief remained seated. Pruitt ignored L. T. and spoke to the chief. "Have you told him?"

"I'm working up to it," said Mackenzie. Chief Mackenzie held up the document he had been studying. "These are deposit records of Ms. Ruby Treatt. Seems her business at the diner has recently increased dramatically. She has, on occasion, been depositing unusually large sums of money into her business account as daily business receipts, then transferring most of the excess into her personal account, then withdrawing it."

"Let me see that." L. T. took the photocopy of Ruby's deposit records and studied it.

Dunphy the banker said, "You'll notice that on June 3 she made a deposit of $19,114.21, then on July 5 she deposited $10,636.19, and on August 4 made a deposit of $21,541.90."

"So what? That diner is packed every time you go in. Everybody eats there. Is it against the law for business to be good?"

"I'm afraid those amounts are way more than Ms. Treatt pulls in from that diner," said the chief.

"Two thousand a day is about average receipts for the diner," said Dunphy. "Twenty-three hundred on a good day, tops."

"Allow me." The mayor, still standing, turned his attention toward L. T. "We know· about your girlfriend." He was standing over L. T., his perfect white teeth exposed in a wide grin. "She's in big trouble. And you know what else? On the morning of each of those large deposits she was seen leaving your residence. I'll bet we can connect you to her little money-laundering scheme and finally rid this town of its village idiot."

It was clear to L. T. that His Honor was taking far too much pleasure in this blindside attack on him. L.T. took it personally. He rose quickly, feeling the venom in his veins setting his skin on fire and threatening to choke him if he didn't expel it immediately. He glared into the eyes of Pruitt momentarily but the mayor didn't back down. "I've had just about enough of you, Randy," L. T. said. He shoved the mayor, forcing him to take a step backward.

"Chief Mackenzie, your sergeant just assaulted me. I want him brought up on charges."

"That's not assault," said L. T. He drew back his right and landed it with force on the teeth of the still-grinning mayor. The mayor slammed against the wall of the office and sank to the floor. Two of his perfect white teeth lay bloodied on the desk of Chief Conrad Mackenzie who sat studying them in silence. "That's assault," said L. T. He turned and headed out the door.

It always came back to that summer of 1991. The entire course of his life changed forever that summer. There he was, a seasoned and professional law enforcement officer with numerous commendations, dignified and respected and destined to be the next chief of WFPD. Willard Paetz was chief back then and he was a man looked up to by all members of the force, especially by Lieutenant L. T. Stafford. But he was up in years and talking seriously about his retirement.

Everyone on the force knew that L. T. was being groomed by Paetz to take over as chief when the latter retired. Then the wheels fell off.

He and Paetz had hit it off from the time L. T. joined the force. They had much in common. Paetz was a veteran of the Korean conflict; Stafford had joined the marines shortly after graduating from White Falls High School and matured rapidly in the jungle combat classrooms of Vietnam. Both men were decorated.

Paetz had grown up in horse country in the rolling hills surrounding Missoula, Montana. As a boy he had always worked at tending horses on several of the neighboring ranches. After the war he thought he was leaving that patient lifestyle behind when he headed east to begin a career in law enforcement. Instead he found northern Ohio's gentle rises and river valleys a pleasant place to ride and could not resist the urge to purchase a small ranch where he could see to the needs of a half dozen quarter horses. Over time his way with horses rubbed off on L. T. Paetz taught him to ride and once a month they would take mounts along a trail that worked its way to the Sandusky River. There they would cook an early Saturday morning breakfast and reflect on lives spent combating the forces of evil.

On the eve of one such ride L. T. was on his way home from a fairly quiet Friday afternoon shift a little after midnight when he heard the radio call for a unit to respond to a single-car traffic accident on River Road. He paid little heed until, as he was about to turn into his driveway the attending officer called in the tag number and driver license. Nothing unusual about the vehicle, a Buick Century registered to Hertz Rental in

Cleveland. But the DL ident took him totally by surprise and he stopped in the street. It was none other than Natalie Pearson. Few outside of White Falls knew her by that name as she had years ago changed her name to Nat Pearce, the Nashville Nightingale and had risen to the rank of superstar in the country music world.

He spun the Jeep in a circle and shot off toward River Road. Then he slowed, wondering what he would say to her, wondering why she had come back after all these years. Even in high school she had been totally focused on making a career of music. L. T. loved to hear her sing and figured she would surely find a way to earn a living at it. But he never once figured she would be this famous. All the unanswered questions suddenly flooded his mind as he wheeled the Jeep through the quiet streets. The biggest one was "Why?" The last time he had seen her he was on leave from the Corps before shipping out to Southeast Asia. He remembered holding her as they vowed to love each other for all time. That was twenty-five years earlier.

The Buick appeared undamaged, having slipped off the asphalt and narrow shoulder into a shallow ditch. Officer Jeff Borden was standing between his patrol car and the Buick talking with the driver under the red, white and blue flashing lights of the vehicles.

Jeff Borden looked toward L. T. and nodded to him as he stepped out of his Jeep and walked toward them. Everyone stopped talking as Natalie and L. T. stared at each other. All of the questions in his mind evaporated as he walked over to her, still gazing into her soft, brown eyes. Neither one smiled. Suddenly the woman threw her arms around L. T. and they embraced for several minutes.

Borden said, "Is there something I should know, Lieutenant?"

"No," said L. T.

"It's good to see you, Luke."

No one had called him that in years. He had been Stafford, L. T. for so long it caught him off guard. He liked how familiar it felt, and how familiar it felt to hold her again. He smiled.

"You just about finished here, Borden?"

"Just waiting for the wrecker."

L. T. looked at her. "You want to get a cup of coffee?"

"Sure."

"Ma'am," said Borden. "I don't think your car's damaged at all, just stuck in that little ditch. What would you like the towing company to do with it when they get it out?"

"I'm staying at the Comfort Inn," she said, still looking at L. T. "Under the name Carter, my mother's maiden name." L. T. took her by the arm and led her to his Jeep. There was a sudden silence as neither one knew which question to ask. Natalie took him by surprise when she reached over and clutched his hand. He thought for a moment of Carolyn waiting at home but knew she would be sound asleep. He often worked through the night when duty required it. He was certain he would not be missed. They drove straight to the Comfort Inn.

The pounding on the glass of the sliding door jolted him upright from the depths of slumber. He looked around at the motel room, the clothes strewn about the floor, Natalie rousing beside him. He tugged on his uniform slacks and zipped them as he drew the corner of the curtain back. It was Borden.

"There's been a terrible accident, Lieutenant. The Chief's been killed. Weren't you supposed to be riding with him this morning?"

Carolyn's car pulled up next to Borden's patrol car.

Natalie was up and dressed and out of his life as suddenly as she had reentered it. The events of that Saturday morning ten years ago sparked a chain reaction. Carolyn ordered him out of their home immediately. Somehow, he was more distraught over the death of Chief Paetz.

There was, of course, an official investigation into the death, but L. T. was not permitted to participate since, because of his intention to be riding with the chief at a time and place that turned out to be the end of the man's life, he needed to be ruled out as a suspect in any possible criminal activity surrounding the incident. The determination of record was conclusive: Chief Paetz died accidentally of massive head injury and severe blood loss as a result of being thrown from his horse and striking his head on a jagged rock protruding from the earth along the trail on which he was riding. Investigating officers said it appeared likely his horse stumbled after stepping on the rock and that spooked it enough to throw its rider.

L. T. didn't buy that official explanation. He had examined the scene on his own looking for some reason to satisfy himself that his friend, a horseman with a lifetime of experience, had actually died accidentally. He had seen the jagged rock and it was bloodied. But to him it didn't seem enough blood to have killed a dog, let alone a man. However, then-councilman Randall Pruitt seemed eager to convince and assure everyone that the event was a tragic accident that likely would not have occurred had Lieutenant L. T. Stafford not found illicit sex more important than protecting his chief.

L. T. had wanted to drill Pruitt back then, and might have, except for the fact that he believed the pompous politician's words to be true and was laden with guilt as a result. So, he didn't ever argue. Soon fellow officers picked up their shovels and helped to heap guilt upon him. That, coupled with the remorse he felt from destroying his marriage drove him deep within himself and caused long bouts of self-examination and criticism.

For a time, his only means of dulling the pain was to attempt to obliterate it with booze. Unfortunately, the numbing effect of the alcohol only served to make him more comfortable with his guilt. It in no way helped him to process and get beyond it. Fellow officers gave him less and less respect, which compounded his negative image of himself and made for fewer and shorter periods of sobriety.

Not long after Conrad Mackenzie of Duluth, Minnesota arrived as new Chief, L. T. found himself suffering the humiliation of having been demoted to the rank of sergeant. The last couple of years L. T. had finally begun to awaken to the fact that most of his wounds were self-inflicted. He had struggled to turn things around. The trouble with sobriety, though, was that it most often kept him from sleeping.

L. T. walked through the front door of the diner at eleven-thirty that morning. Ruby was in the kitchen scooping coleslaw into small, white china bowls. The tinkling of the bell made her glance through the order window and when she saw he was out of uniform she dropped a bowl of coleslaw that hit the floor with a clatter. L. T. took a seat at the counter. Ruby's head poked through the order window.

"Jesus. It's true?"

"Yep, I'm officially retired."

Ruby came through the swinging door, poured him a cup of coffee and leaned on the counter in front of him.

"Retired my ass," she whispered. "You really punched out the mayor, didn't you?"

"Oh, you heard about our retirement meeting," he said without emotion.

"Why'd you do it, L. T.? You were so close. Why'd you let him sucker you like that?"

"Ruby, there's a problem."

"For real, L. T. You're screwed. What are you going to do now?"

"Ruby listen to me. You've got a problem."

"Sure do. I've got an unemployed tenant. How you going to pay your rent?" She winked at him. "Don't worry, Hon. We'll think of something."

"You're being investigated."

"What? Don't be silly."

He stared back at her, his face without expression.

"You're serious," she said. "Investigated for what? Cereal in the burgers?"

47

Just then Orville Hennessey, father of L.T.'s ex-wife, entered the restaurant. L. T. turned to see who came in and Hennessey shook his head.

"I suppose you'll be moving on, Stafford," he said. "Nothing much to keep you here now, is there? Unless, of course, you find yourself facing criminal charges for this brutal attack on the mayor. I imagine a civil suit will follow. Though God knows you haven't a thing worth suing for."

That's right, L. T. thought. The old bastard's daughter and her husband the mayor already cleaned me out ten years ago. But he didn't answer Hennessey's rantings.

"They should have run your ass out of town when you let Chief Paetz die."

Ruby waved at Priscilla to go and take the old man's order. He told her to just bring coffee as he'd lost his appetite.

"Seems like you might have stirred up some long-forgotten troubles," Ruby said.

"Most of my troubles," L. T. said softly, "Will never be forgotten."

The phone rang and Ruby marched into the kitchen to answer it. She returned a moment later with a puzzled look.

"What's up?" L. T. asked.

"That was Bertha, my sister-in-law. You've met my brother Arnie, from New York. He comes in here once in a while when he's on the semi. He works dad's farm but sometimes he trucks for extra money. He took a run to Florida last week but didn't show up to pick up his load on Saturday morning. My sister-in-law just called to see if I'd heard from him. He's never missed a pickup. I wonder where he could be."

Chapter Five

The Vernon Wheatley Citrus Packing House of Indian River sat on the west side of A1A a mile north of Vero Beach and across the street from a strip mall with a real-estate office, a half-dozen stores and a Denny's restaurant. Carla leaned a hip against a post supporting the roof that overhung the loading dock and watched as the last stack of grapefruit-filled cartons was slip-sheeted onto a pallet inside the rear of the Great Dane. She wore tight jeans and a pale blue tank top with no bra, a combination that always got her trailer loaded quickly. When the forklift backed clear of the trailer she moved in and secured a load lock behind the stacks to keep the last row of boxes from shifting during the trip north.

"That's eleven-hundred cartons," the shipper said, handing her the bill of lading. "That's about forty-five hundred pounds more than most folks will haul in a load. You feeling lucky, Miss?"

"Naw," she drawled, "Just damn pretty. If you were running a scale house, would you cite me for overweight?"

"No, ma'am, I sure wouldn't."

She just winked at him.

"If you pull it away from the dock, I'll shut the trailer doors for you." He couldn't keep his eyes off the outline of her nipples.

"Thanks, partner." She smiled and his face broke into a broad grin. Being a pretty woman in a man's job sure saved a lot of work, Carla thought to herself. She let her hips sway as she walked toward the cab of her new Kenworth. Clutching the grab handle, she hoisted herself up and in and fired the engine, slipped the transmission into low gear, released the parking brake and idled ahead ten feet. Her eyes went to the left mirror as she waited for the shipper to close up the trailer and when he waved she rolled the rig toward the driveway. She faced the strip mall and was about to swing out onto A1A when something made her hit the air brakes. A black man in a yellow Hawaiian shirt and red leather skull cap walked out of the Denny's, climbed onto an old, yellow Shovelhead Harley and fired it up with a roar.

Marlin was rolling just a few miles north of Gainsville when it hit him this time. He could usually get a couple days up the road before he started talking to Mickey, but he hadn't slept much since the events of Friday night and was getting fatigued early. Whenever Marlin grew road-weary he would slip back into the scene. It had started out as his favorite fantasy, looking over at the empty passenger seat and imagining Mickey Rourke riding along as his co-driver. Mickey was always in shit and that made him Marlin's Hollywood idol.

In the story, Mickey has pissed off so many Hollywood big shots that nobody wants to work with him anymore and he leaves town all down and out, having lost everything. Marlin drops a load in L.A. and heads south on the Pacific Coast Highway to pick up a haul back in San Diego. But he's hungry and has to stop at a diner in Laguna Beach. He's about to enter the restaurant when the front door comes flying off with some dude attached to it. He peers in cautiously and sees none other than his all-time hero taking on four wise asses and Marlin can see that Mickey's in deep shit. So, he wades in and takes a stance alongside Mickey and the two of them start cleaning up the place. They wreak havoc in the diner but get the upper hand and are about to finish the foursome when the sound of sirens splits the air. Marlin knows Mickey will do time if he takes a ride over this so he grabs his arm and pulls him out of there. They jump into Marlin's rig and are rolling south and laughing their butts off by the time the law arrives. Of course, Mickey is fascinated by the life Marlin leads, traveling all the time and the skill with which he handles such a huge machine while making it look easy. By the time they reach San Diego, Mickey is behind the wheel and totally hooked on trucking so Marlin gives him a job as co-driver.

Now Marlin slips in and out of the fantasy whenever he needs help to stay awake. Sometimes he's talking to Mickey without even realizing he's not really there. If he isn't too tired, Marlin simply says things aloud to the empty seat, while Mickey's half of the dialogue plays itself out within his mind. Sometimes he doesn't even have Mickey's thoughts, just sits lecturing the empty seat about the finer details of the matters of interstate trucking. On the occasions when he's been running too long and too hard, though, both sides of the conversation are audible as Marlin plays both parts. Today he just started right into it as Mickey.

Mickey: "So who's running this outfit?"

Marlin: "I am, bet your ass."

Mickey: "Ha," he laughed. "Your sister stomped all over your authority this weekend. You ain't Jack Shit from what I seen."

Marlin: "Don't you worry about it. I'm in charge."

Mickey: "Then how come you're driving this bucket of bolts and she's cruising in a brand new KW?"

Marlin: "She got the new truck because I allowed her to have it."

Mickey: "Right. She's all over you man and you know it. Only reason you're alive at all is because Carla allowed it by saving your ass. She killed that guy. You couldn't do it, could you?"

Marlin: "Course not, the asshole had the drop on me."

Mickey: "Don't you watch the movies man? Somebody gets the drop on you, you look for his weakness and take advantage of it. If that was me, I'd have disarmed him in seconds, shoved that revolver so far up his ass he'd be spitting bullets. You were chickenshit and she saved your ass."

Marlin: "That fucking bitch."

Mickey: "You know she's never going to let you live it down. You know she's always going to have it over you. She can ride your ass now and get anything she wants. Carla's running this outfit now."

Marlin's hands were twisting on the steering wheel; he was burning with anger.

Marlin: "I'll handle it, I can take care of her."

Mickey: Yeah, right. Let me ask you something. Who made the decision to dump the dude in the river?"

Marlin: "Fuck you Mickey!" He slapped the steering wheel.

Mickey: "So, what are you going to do about her?"

Marlin: "I'll think of something."

Mickey: "You'll think of something. That's it? You'll think of something? Listen boss you've got a real situation here. You know what happens to a dog that kills a chicken? That dog gets the taste of blood, that's all he wants to eat. He can't stop killing chickens; he's totally out of control. Know how they cure that? They kill the fucking dog."

Marlin: "What are you saying?"

Mickey: "You saw her man. Killing that dude was the biggest thrill of her life. It was like sex for her. She's got to have more and she'll go looking for it. Only one way to stop her."

Marlin: "Are you saying what I think you're saying?"

Mickey: "I'm saying if you don't get control of her fast you'll have only one way to stop her: kill her."

Marlin: "No. No, she may be spun but she's my sister. I practically raised her myself. No, I've got a better idea."

Mickey: "I'm all ears, dude."

Marlin: "She's in control because she thinks she's the only one that can kill someone and get away with it. She'll have nothing if I kill somebody too."

By the time the sun had crossed the highway to shine on her left shoulder Carla was getting the urge to stop for supper, though she didn't feel much like eating. Her eyes kept flitting to the mirror. She had to squint as she peered toward the sun but the reflection of that old, yellow Harley still held within the glass. It's rider sat hunched over and clinging to the handlebars, determined to keep no more than a few feet from the shiny rear doors of the stainless steel Great Dane. He had followed her all the way from the packinghouse in Vero Beach, past Jacksonville and into Georgia and he gave no sign of stopping. Carla ran the fingers of her right hand nervously through her short black hair then reached for the shift lever. She eased up on the fuel, slipped the stick back a cog to drop the thirteen-speed into twelfth gear, and let the engine brake slow the rig, the exhaust barking loudly from twin chrome stacks as the truck slowed to take the ramp for the Brunswick exit. She wheeled the giant rig into the truck stop and watched as the motorcyclist parked in front of the restaurant, dismounted and entered the building. She could no longer see him, but she knew the black man was watching her as she shut the rig down and headed inside.

She looked for him when she entered the restaurant but didn't see him. She took a booth next to the windows and as the waitress set a steaming cup of coffee and a menu before her a voice said, "Make it two." He slid into the seat opposite her and grinned.

"You following me?" Carla didn't return the smile.

"I'd say that fact ought to be crystal clear in your mind by now, Sugar."

"Don't call me Sugar. And if you don't go away, the State Troopers will find you a room for the night, maybe longer. You heard of the stalking laws?"

"I'd love to see you in stockings and nothing else. Mmm, lord have mercy."

"That's enough bullshit, I'm calling the cops." She started to rise, but he clutched her wrist.

"I don't think you want to do that."

She sat back down and he let go her wrist. "My name's Elvis." He held out his hand to shake but she just glared fire at him. "Elvis Wood. I'm a commercial fisherman by trade. Sort of, that is. I don't do no deep-sea fishing or ocean trawling or anything like that, but I make enough to keep my hog on the road by supplying fresh-water mullet to a couple soul-food restaurant establishments around Dade City."

"Where the hell you run a commercial fishing boat in Dade? It's nowhere near the water."

"Didn't say I ran a fishing boat. I set trot lines in the Coochee Coochee."

Carla's face turned white as the clouds but she said nothing.

"Yeah, I know you know what I'm talking about. There I was, Friday night, setting my trotlines like usual just downriver from the 98 Bridge. Along comes this eighteen-wheeler, stops right in the middle of the bridge and douses the lights. I hear the trailer doors open, a bunch of grunting and groaning, then a big splash. You are never going to guess what I caught in my lines that night."

Carla sat frozen, listening to his monologue.

"First I reckoned hell, they just ditching some trash. Then it snagged my lines and I had to drag it to the bank. When I saw that poor dead slob, I made for my scooter and followed y'all with no lights burning. Once I seen where y'all lived I came back, helped myself to the guy's wallet. Hey, I figure he's checked out, ain't no way he needs it. Then – you ain't going to believe this shit, Mama – then I fishes a screwdriver out of his back. Nice screwdriver. Matches the one your boyfriend loaned me Saturday morning. It's outside in my saddlebag. What you make of all that?"

"Guess you got it all figured out, huh Elvis."

"Bet your lily-white ass, Sugar."

"So what's next, you call the cops or you fucking blackmail me?"

"Naw, I'm on your side, Sugar. I just reckon this is like free rent for old Elvis. Like you go to McDonald's drive-through, spill a hot coffee in your crotch and sue their ass for three million. Right place, right time. Know what I mean?"

"You want to sue me. What, I messed up your fishing? What kind of bullshit is that?"

"Naw, you got it all wrong. I just figure I'm about due to move up in the world. I reckon I could make a sweet living as an interstate truck driver. Travel all the time, see the country, make shitloads of cash. I'd be your new partner, Sugar."

"Tell me something Elvis. After you hauled that slob out of the river and stole his wallet, what did you do with him?"

His eyes narrowed. "What you mean?"

"I mean, did you put him back into the river?"

"The hell I want to do that for?"

Carla leaned over the table and spoke in whispers. "So the gators could eat the evidence. So the cops can't ever find a body so they never look for a killer."

"Ain't no gators in that stretch of the river, woman. Closest gators down river about five miles where the water pools and stands at the S bend."

"Well, Einstein. Do you think if you put him back in the water he would go up river? What did you do with him?"

"I left him on the bank in the tall weeds there. He's outa sight."

"Think maybe you ought to go back there tonight and help him back into the water so nobody comes looking for you?"

He stared across the table at her.

"You handled that body. They got all kinds of scientific shit they do to dead folks nowadays to tell how they died and who did it. Don't you watch TV? What am I saying? Of course you don't learn that stuff on the African-American Network."

"You're jiving me, woman. You just want me to get rid of that body so they don't come looking for you and your boyfriend. It was your boyfriend did that dude, don't try to hang that shit on me."

Carla nodded. "You're right. He did it. And to tell you the truth, he hasn't been treating me all that good lately. But I don't want to see him spend his life in prison. Look, if you want to be my partner, you've got to give me something here."

"Like what?"

"Like an act of good faith."

"I'm listening."

"You've got to understand, I thought this body was gone by now, eaten by gators. Now you tell me it's laying on the riverbank near Dade, and that could be a problem. I'm heading north and I can't turn around and head back with this load on. I need you to put that guy back in the water after dark."

"You seem awful interested in getting me to go back to the scene of your boyfriend's crime. You could be fixing to spring a trap on me."

58

"You're right. I am interested in getting you to go back to that riverbank. Because if you don't, there might not be a trucking business for you to be a partner in. If my boyfriend goes down, I'll go down with him. There goes your free rent." She reached across and lightly touched the back of his hand with her fingertips. She smiled at him for the first time. "Besides, you want me to like you." She slid out of the seat. "Come on. I'll show you the truck you'll be driving."

Carla unlocked and opened the driver's door, then walked around and climbed in through the passenger door.

"What are you waiting for?" she called out to the black man standing beside the truck.

Elvis slid into the driver's seat, wrapped two large hands about opposite sides of the leather-covered steering wheel and let out a long whistle of approval. He peered out over the long, straight nose of the Kenworth, imagining himself cruising the Interstate from coast to coast. He glanced in the left mirror, then the right, then he slowly took in the complex detail of the instrument panel, reading aloud the name of each gauge and control.

"Air pressure, oil pressure, oil temperature, coolant temperature." He moved the air-ride seat up and down, feeling it glide smoothly, gauging its firmness. He ran his fingers along the naugahyde door panel, admiring the texture.

Carla slid from her seat and stepped into the sleeper compartment, flipping on the interior lights.

"Ain't this just the cat's ass?" she cooed.

Elvis swung in his seat to look at her but couldn't speak. The driver's lounge housed an oak dresser and matching dinette table, upper and lower berths, padded naugahyde walls and a skylight. He shifted out of the seat and crept into the lounge.

"Have a seat." Carla pointed to the lower berth and he sank onto it. "So, what do you think? Think you can go back to Dade and get rid of our little problem?"

"Oh, yeah. I'm on it, Sugar. Consider the dude disappeared."

She tugged her tank top over her head, put her hands on his shoulders and pushed him backward into a prone position. Then she slid atop him and said, "Guess we better seal the partnership."

It was dark when Carla rolled the big rig out of the truck stop and watched the headlight of the yellow Harley in the mirrors. Elvis took the southbound ramp, Carla the northbound. When his taillight disappeared in the distance she reached for her cellular phone and punched the emergency number for the Georgia Highway Patrol.

"Nine-one-one emergency service," said the operator. "What is your name and the nature of your emergency?"

Carla gave an alias and told a story about overhearing a black motorcyclist say he had killed a man on the bank of the Withlacoochee River near the US98 Bridge outside Dade City, Florida. She told the trooper that he had stabbed the man with a screwdriver a few days earlier, and that he was now heading south on Interstate 95 on a yellow Harley-Davidson, and included the license number. She ended the call before any questions could be asked.

Chapter Six

At Ruby's request, L. T. made a few phone calls in search of her overdue brother. He started with Bertha Perkins, Arnold's wife who expressed concern that her usually dependable husband had not been heard from since Friday afternoon. In the next breath she told L. T. that if he found Arnold he was to let him know in no uncertain terms that he had better get his fat ass home in time to take the corn off as she wasn't about to do it herself. Furthermore, he best not come trucking in with another dose of the clap lest he should become the next John Bobbit. Then she gave him the number of Gary Turner, the owner/operator whose truck was missing along with Perkins.

Turner also indicated that Perkins was known among the local owner/operators as being very reliable. He had never known him to be late, let alone miss a pickup. Worried that something must have happened to the farmer, he urged L.T. to find Arnold and his missing rig. He then passed along the number of Claude Primeau, the manager and Chief Dispatcher at NY Truck Brokers.

"I seen it once, I seen it a hundred times," said Primeau. "It's always these fill-in drivers. You send them down to the Bikini State, they find out it's forever warm there and they start gypsying."

"What do you mean?" asked L. T.

"Look, Officer. This is trucking, it ain't rocket science. Give me a chimpanzee and thirty minutes of his time and I'll give you a truck driver. You send some young buck to Florida in a shiny, new rig and all he sees is sunshine and women in thongs and he wants to stay there, maybe just an extra day or so. So he calls a local broker, gets himself a load of citrus to Knoxville, picks up a check. He's about to double back to paradise when he sees a note on the truck stop bulletin board. So he goes to Spartanburg, gets a load of apples to New Orleans, picks up a check. Next he loads rice for Atlanta, picks up a check. Before you know it, he's painted over the name on the truck, stolen a set of tags and he's making a mighty fine living without ever making a truck payment. Ought to be a law against it."

"There is," said L. T. "Several, in fact. Only this isn't a young man with no responsibilities, this is a sixty-year-old man with a wife and a farm, both of which need tending. He's also a man who is known to be dependable."

"Fine, don't take it from me, talk to Turner, the guy that owns the missing rig. He tells me this farmer's wife is as handsome as the southern end of his northbound ox team and just as broad. Give a poor slob dirt farmer an opportunity to see the country in a shiny, new motor home and a means of making moolah doing it and you got yourself one missing truck and one happy ex-farmer. I'll guarantee you he feels like he's broke jail, we'll never see his sorry ass or his friend's truck again."

L.T. called Gary Turner again for a description of the rig. The truck's owner deduced that since the load was delivered in Tampa on Friday afternoon and the pickup was to be made a couple hours north of there at Brooksville, the truck was likely somewhere between the two points. He dismissed Primeau's theory of gypsying, saying Perkins would never stay away from his farm for long. He went on to say that Perkins' favorite layover was the truck stop at Wildwood, just down the road from Brooksville. But Turner had already heard from another driver who popped by the truck stop to look for his rig and there was no sign of it.

He made one final call – to the Florida Highway Patrol just to see if Arnold Perkins had actually been reported missing. He had. L.T. decided to identify himself as a police officer in the hope that it would make the FHP a little freer with information than they might ordinarily be. What the hell, he figured, it had only been hours since he left the WFPD anyway. Trooper Warden Trout very courteously reviewed the details of the file but made no secret of the fact that a missing truck and driver had not generated a great deal of interest with the State Police. According to Trout it was not that unusual for a trucker to run away from home while in the State of Florida. But he promised to call if any news broke. L.T. gave the number of his brand new cell phone for call back in the event of developments.

About mid-afternoon L.T. took a break and drove his six-year-old Ford Explorer over to Griffith Auto and Truck Repair to ask his friend Kendall Griffith why the CHECK ENGINE light on the instrument panel had been lit for the best part of a month. The eight-bay garage was full of everything from compact cars to farm tractors, with men working in every stall. L. T. strolled into the heavy truck bay where he found the lanky Griffith standing next to the engine of a longnose Freightliner, about to remove the turbocharger. L. T. told him about his problem.

"I'm sorry, L. T., but there's just no way I can look at it today. I got the guys on overtime now and we just can't seem to keep up."

"Nice to see someone's making a fortune."

"What the hell's that supposed to mean?" Griffith threw his wrench down. It clanged and bounced across the concrete floor. He turned to face L. T. "Look at this place." He waved an arm. "Eight bays I can't afford the overhead on, a dozen technicians working two shifts and they all want a raise, and partners threatening bodily harm if I don't increase the return on their investment. And people like you come in and assume I'm overcharging them just to get fat. I'm about fed up with it all." He heaved the turbocharger toward his chest, pulling it free from the exhaust manifold and carried it to the workbench where he let it slide from his hands to fall on the steel table top with a loud clatter. He stood examining the worn component, ignoring L. T.

"What partners? You've never had a partner in your life."

"Forget it," he said, still looking at the turbocharger. "I was just letting off steam. Just forget it." Griffith began to disassemble the failed unit. L.T. turned and walked out.

L.T. let out a long, slow breath. He could feel another sleepless night coming on, and another wave of depression with it as the walls began to close in on him. This thing with Ruby and the alleged money laundering, then her brother disappears. Old man

Hennessey fires a couple of rounds at him and rubs salt in old wounds around the death of Chief Paetz that happened ten years ago. But worst of all he had finally given in to his urge to sucker punch Randy Pruitt and it did just enough damage to likely result in a felony assault charge. At the very least, he had already been made aware that it had cost him his badge.

Of course, it was just what Pruitt wanted, L.T. knew that and it made him want to take another poke at the asshole. But even the first one wasn't worth it. It was a hell of an end to a lifetime career of law enforcement. It was about eight in the evening and the September sun was setting as he trudged up the stairs to his apartment. He fished the key from the bird feeder and caught the faint glow of a cigarette in the semi-darkness of his living room as he slid the key into the deadbolt lock. He flung the door open and instinctively reached for his gun but his hand came up empty as he burst through the door.

"Jesus, is that your finger or are you just glad to see me?" Ruby said smugly. She remained seated on the sofa.

He switched on the overhead light, saw that she was naked, then switched it off again. He flopped on the sofa next to her.

"Ruby, this is really not a good time…"

"Shut up and just hold me." She butted her cigarette and slid her arms around him. He pulled her close. They both sighed and sat a long time in each other's arms without speaking.

Marlin was still firing remarks at the empty passenger seat, but with much less frequency. The morning sun was breaking over a hill to the east of Marietta, Georgia and Marlin always found dawn to be the most difficult time to stay awake. He had stopped for a nap just south of Macon about two this morning, but was badly in need of more sleep. The broken white lines on the gray-black asphalt flashed by in an endless stream, hypnotizing him so that his head would slip down toward his chest until the pressure on the back of his neck awakened him and caused him to jerk it upright, blinking his eyes to try to make them stay open. The tractor wheels edged over the line, creeping into the center lane as Marlin struggled to remain conscious. A sharp blast from the horn of a black BMW slapped him awake and he yanked the steering wheel to the right to avoid running over the car. The driver's arm shot out the window, middle finger extended.

Marlin: "Would you look at this smart ass?" He glanced over at the empty passenger seat.

Mickey: "Do you believe that motherfucker? Almost rams us then shoots us the bird. Does he have a death wish or what?"

Marlin: "He shouldn't have done that." Marlin leaned on the accelerator, black smoke belched from the twin chrome stacks, the roar of the Caterpillar engine gained a few decibels, but the drag of the heavily laden trailer kept the rig from surging forward.

Mickey: "Come on, put your foot into it. Let's catch that asshole and show him who owns this fucking road."

Marlin: "For your information my foot is flat on the floor. This is an eighteen-wheeler, it ain't the space shuttle. And it don't accelerate like a BMW. And no fucking way will it pull a hill like one."

Mickey: "But he's getting away. We can't let him shit on us and just take off. Let's teach him a lesson."

Marlin: "Don't worry, I have a better idea. For now, we'll keep him in sight."

Marlin was suddenly wide-awake and could feel the adrenaline surging, his hands tightly gripping the oversize steering wheel to reduce the sudden shaking. Traffic thinned as the distance from Marietta increased. He gradually urged the truck's speed upward, hitting engine governor speed with ease going down the hills, then mashing the accelerator early as the truck shot into the next uphill grade. The technique relied on generating excess downhill momentum to reduce speed loss on the uphill grades. It didn't mean he could keep up with the BMW but after twenty minutes had gone by he could still pick out the glint of the sun on its clear-coat shine, saw it's right turn indicator flashing amber in the distance and knew the driver was taking the exit ramp at the Route 411 junction.

The Kenworth followed a couple of minutes later. It barked along the off-ramp, the sound of its engine brake reverberating through the red clay hills as the big rig bled off speed. Marlin scanned the area, spotted the black car at a filling station across 411 on the southbound side. He eased the truck onto the right of way and took the first left, which led down a wide drive to the rear of the same filling station where the diesel fuel pumps were located. Air brakes hissed loudly as Marlin brought the truck to a stop between the rows of pumps and signaled the attendant with both thumbs up. A young black man ran a hose to the polished aluminum fuel tank on the left side of the truck, switched it on, then circled the tractor and ran another hose into the right tank. Marlin climbed down from the rig, opened the compartment beneath the sleeper and fished a small knife from his toolbox. He told the attendant to fill the reefer tank also, then headed around the building toward the front of the station.

The driver of the BMW finished fueling it and went inside to pay. Marlin walked past the far side of the car and stopped near its rear wheel. He bent down, pretending to tie his shoe. After glancing around to make sure no one was looking, he deftly carved a slice in the valve stem of the right rear tire, listened as it hissed gently, then rose and walked on, circling the building until he arrived back at his truck. He climbed in and waited patiently as the fuel continued to fill his tanks.

It took ten minutes more to fuel the truck and pay. When they were rolling again, Mickey started right in.

Mickey: "Jesus, we could've had him right there. You just let him go. Are you chickenshit, or what?"

Marlin: "Don't you fucking call me chickenshit, Mickey. I'm the one who saved your ass in Laguna. Remember? I'm the one who gave you a job when they ran your ass out of Hollywood. Don't you fucking forget it."

Mickey: "But you just let him go."

Marlin: "Let him go? No. Just played out a little line, is all. He'll be waiting for us up the road where things are a little quieter."

Ten minutes later Marlin spotted the black BMW pulled off to the side halfway down a hill. The driver knelt beside the right rear tire cranking the handle on a jack to lift the flat tire off the warm asphalt. Marlin applied the brakes and eased the rig off the driving lanes onto the shoulder and prepared to stop. He looked over at the passenger seat and grinned.

Mickey: "I ain't believing this shit. You son of a bitch, Marlin. You knew it all the time. You slash his tire? Stick it with an ice pick?"

Marlin: "Told you I had him where I wanted him."

The big rig shuddered to a hissing stop just a few feet from the rear of the car. It's driver, a man of about 40, clean-shaven with slick hair and a crisp white shirt and black tie removed the flat right rear and laid it on its side. Marlin jumped down and hurried around to the BMW driver.

"Can I give you a hand, sir?" He walked straight over to where the car's lug nuts lay in the upside down wheel cover. Marlin accidentally kicked the wheel cover and scattered it and the wheel nuts under the raised automobile.

"What the hell are you doing?" the man cried. "Do all you dumb truckers have shit for brains? Jesus, what the fuck am I supposed to do now? I've got a meeting in Chattanooga at ten and I can't fucking miss it." He waved his arms and shook his head.

"Sorry, mister," Marlin said convincingly. "I probably got something in the truck I can fish them out with."

"Leave it," said the BMW owner. "Just leave it and get back in that dinosaur and never cross my path again. Got it?"

Marlin turned and walked quietly back to the truck. He climbed in and sat behind the wheel with the engine running, watching light southbound traffic coming at him, eyeing in the mirror even lighter northbound traffic, and delighting at the sight of the perplexed executive with a flat tire, a perfectly good spare, and no wheel nuts. After about five minutes of peering around and under the car, the driver began to remove his shirt and tie. Next, he got down on his belly and began to drag himself under the BMW to retrieve the lug nuts. Marlin took a last look at traffic, jammed the truck into low and released the clutch, hitting the accelerator at the same time. The truck surged forward on the downhill grade, rammed the shiny, black BMW and knocked it off its jack. The car fell with a loud bang and a pair of legs in neatly pressed black slacks shook wildly for a moment as electrodes misfired deep within the man's brain. Then they grew still. Marlin put the rig in reverse to give the truck room to clear the disabled car and its dead driver, and then rolled on down the hill heading north.

Ruby spent the night but was downstairs in the diner when L.T. dragged himself out of bed around seven. He wasn't sure how long he had slept but knew it couldn't have been more than a couple hours. Hennessey's comments about the Chief kept gnawing away at him throughout the night. Most of the black hours were spent beating himself up over the fact that he had always suspected something amiss in the circumstances surrounding the death of his chief but had never done a thing about it. That, and the way that his career had suddenly just ended became a heavy load for him to tote.

He poured a cup from the coffee pot Ruby had fixed earlier. Before he could sit down he heard the ring of his new cell phone and went to retrieve it from his trousers crumpled on the living room floor. It was Trooper Warden Trout of the Florida Highway Patrol.

"Bet you didn't expect to hear from me so soon. I have news but I'm afraid it's not good. Your friend, Mr. Perkins has met with foul play." He paused.

"You've found his body? You've identified him?"

"We have a fingerprint match on the Driver's License."

"What about cause of death?" L.T. quickly scratched notes as the trooper spoke.

"We're waiting on the M.E.'s report. That is, the Sheriff's Department in Pasco County is. They're handling the investigation. I spoke with Sheriff Henry, though, and he tells me there was a puncture wound in the upper torso that went clean through."

"Somebody shot him."

"Sheriff Henry didn't think so. Said it looked more like stabbed. He hopes to know more when the M.E. is finished, and when his deputies have thoroughly completed their interview process with the suspect."

"They have the assailant in custody? Already? Jesus, what was the motive?"

"I'm afraid that's all I know, Sergeant. You'll have to check with Sheriff Henry." He gave L.T. the number.

L.T. thought about going down to the diner to inform Ruby of her brother's demise. He considered calling her to ask her to come up so that he could break it to her a little more gently in private. That seemed the better way to handle it but he decided to place a call to the Pasco County Sheriff's Department first. He was surprised to be put through to Sheriff Branford Henry at such an early hour.

"Criminals don't work nine to five, Mr. Stafford. Neither do we. What can I do for you?"

"It's Sergeant Stafford, White Falls Police Department in Ohio. I understand you have recovered the remains of Arnold Perkins."

"And just what is your interest in the life and / or death of the late Mr. Perkins? According to his D.L. he was a resident of Rutland Center, New York. Why are the police in White Falls, Ohio looking for our homicide victim?"

"I'm not actually calling on an official police matter, Sheriff. I happen to be a friend of the family and am inquiring on their behalf." L.T. was trying his best not to sound annoyed.

"Well, if you are who you say you are, then you ought to know we can't release any details of this case, including identification of the deceased, until next of kin has been notified. Since you are not next of kin, I reckon that means this conversation is over. On the other hand, if you had told me you were calling on official business I'd have a different answer for you."

L.T. sucked in a breath. "All right, I'm calling on official police business."

"Go to hell." The line went dead.

L.T. was still staring at the phone when Ruby came through the door.

"You didn't need to get all dressed up for me, L.T."

He looked down at his bare chest and white jockey shorts and started to get up. "Ruby, you better sit down."

"Not now, Hon'. I just came up to tell you one of Kendall Griffith's mechanic's found him dead when they opened the shop this morning. Hung himself."

He sank back onto the sofa.

Chapter Seven

Carla wolfed down grits, eggs and biscuits at a truckstop on I-77 near Statesville, North Carolina, then slipped into the drivers' lounge to update her log book and to use the internet service to check traffic and road construction heading north. Afterward she brought up the web site of a Tampa television station to check the news headlines back home. She found the item she was looking for: an unidentified black man from Dade City had been arrested in connection with the disappearance and death of a missing truck driver from New York. Carla sang a country tune all the way back to her truck. She was about to climb in and head north but was suddenly overcome with the urge to tell Marlin the good news. She headed back to the lounge and used a pay phone to call his cell number.

"Sears Refrigerated Transport," he answered.

"Hey."

"Hey yourself, Sis. Have I got some news for you."

"Never mind that, I've got something absolutely huge to tell you. Get to a land line and call me at the truckstop in Statesville." She hung up before he could utter another word.

"Ruby, listen to me. I need to talk to you about your brother," L.T. said.

She studied his face for a moment noting the firm set of his jaw, the wrinkle in his brow. But it was the darkness in his eyes that seemed to hold a hint of sadness and caused her to sink into the chair opposite him in the living room of his apartment. She looked down at his clothes strewn about the floor but took no notice of them or the fact that he was still clad only in jockey shorts. Ruby could not look into his eyes again for she knew they held the worst possible news. Her hands went to her face and covered her own eyes but could not conceal the quiet flood of tears.

L.T. got up from the sofa and moved to stand beside her and gently stroke her hair. "I'm sorry, Ruby," he half-whispered. "I don't have all the details but the police in Florida have discovered that Arnold has died. They have recovered his body near a place called Dade City." He took a breath. "They say he met with foul play."

"He was murdered?" she asked, without uncovering her eyes.

"Yes."

"Do they need me to identify him?"

"No." He thought it an odd question and wanted to say so but he began to find it difficult to form words as he felt her sorrow creep over him. He had found himself in the position of notifying next of kin numerous times before and it was never pleasant but he had always been able to disassociate himself from the families of accident or crime victims. This time, however, was different. He could not escape the sudden urge to share in Ruby's loss, to try in some way to lighten her load, though he had no idea how he might do that.

"Does Bertha know?" Ruby asked.

"The police in Dade City will be contacting her shortly."

"I guess I figured all along something bad had happened to him. Otherwise he'd never let us worry like this. But I just don't get it, L.T. Who would want to kill Arnie? He wouldn't hurt a fly."

The sound of a rap on the door kept L.T. from answering. He glanced toward the window to see two uniformed officers standing on the porch and he reached for his trousers to slip them on before answering the knock. He assumed they had come to notify Ruby of her brother's death so he opened the door as soon as he was presentable.

"Morning, L.T.," said Jason Ferguson. . "We're looking for Ms. Treat. Priscilla, downstairs at the diner, said she was up here."

L.T. waved them in. He wanted to ask about Kendall Griffith but knew it was not a good time for that. He stood clear as the officers entered his living room.

"Ms. Treat, we need you to go downtown to the station with us to answer a few questions, please."

Ruby looked at L.T.

"Is that necessary?" L.T. asked. "I mean, the guy died in Florida, there's a homicide investigation being carried out there. What could you possibly expect Ruby to know about it?"

"What guy died in Florida, Sarge? Ms. Treat, are you involved in a homicide?"

"No. Don't you know? What the hell are you guys here for?" Ruby looked puzzled, as did L.T.

"Aren't you guys here about her brother?" L.T. asked.

"No, Sarge. She's wanted for questioning in another matter."

"What other matter?" asked L.T., his voice a few decibels louder at their invasion of Ruby's privacy in her time of sorrow.

"Afraid we can't say, L.T. Chief says we have to bring her in. Ma'am, if you could come along willingly we can avoid the use of restraints."

"Restraints?" L.T. shouted. "Jesus, you want to cuff her? For what?"

Ferguson's partner unbuttoned the snap on his holster and gripped the butt of his pistol in readiness. "Don't make this difficult, Sarge," he said. "We know you've committed one assault already." The officer motioned to Ruby to move out the door. "You'll have to come with us, Ma'am."

L.T.'s jaw dropped at the threat of force. He stood silent as the officers escorted Ruby, still wearing her waitress uniform, down the stairs to their police car.

"I'll get April Brewster," L.T. called after her. "She'll get this sorted out for you." He dialed the lawyer's home number. Brewster agreed to call WFPD to find out what was going on and said she would attend at the questioning if she felt it necessary.

L.T. decided to head for Griffith's garage to see if anyone there could shed some light on what had caused his friend to kill himself. He arrived to find the place staked out with yellow tape. A couple of mechanics stood outside talking with two men in suits that L.T. didn't recognize. No other garage employees were visible, inside or out. Lieutenant Emerson Weaver, ten years his junior, appeared to be in charge of the investigation. Two younger officers were examining the engine bay where a chain dangled from a block and tackle mounted on a steel beam above them. An electric motor powered the device with a control box attached to a long cable that allowed it to be operated from anywhere in the room. It was used for lifting heavy engines in and out of automobiles. Weaver spotted L.T. and walked out to meet him in the parking lot.

"You can't be here, Stafford," the policeman said with his hands up, palms outward.

"Kendall was a friend of mine. I want to know what happened to him. That's all." He spoke calmly and quietly.

Weaver stared at him for a moment, then pointed toward the engine bay. "We're satisfied that Mr. Griffith stood in the center of that room, wrapped that chain about his neck, and pushed the button that hoisted the chain and himself upward. A simple suicide."

"No suicide is ever simple." L.T. took a few steps toward the open garage door to the bay where the body had been found. Weaver followed. "Who was the last person to see him alive?" asked L.T. "What was the time of death?" He studied the scene. "Did you dust that remote control for prints?"

"Apparently no one told you," said Weaver. "You're out of law enforcement. But don't worry, Stafford. We still have one or two competent officers who can stay sober long enough to investigate a suicide."

L.T. let it pass. "Look, I knew this man. I just can't believe he would ever kill himself. Why don't you get a forensics team down here from Toledo?"

An unmarked police car wheeled onto the parking lot and stopped near them. Chief Conrad Mackenzie stepped out and joined them.

"What are you doing here?" said Mackenzie.

"Chief, this could be a crime scene. Why aren't your people gathering evidence?"

"Go home, L.T. Leave the detective work to real police officers." He looked at Weaver. "Are you about finished here?"

"Just a few more minutes, Chief. I thought we should get a print man down here to check that remote control. Just to rule out anything suspicious." He glanced in L.T.'s direction acknowledging the logic in his suggestion.

"Don't tell me you've been listening to Stafford." He shook his head. "The poor slob killed himself. Wouldn't you be depressed if you faced the prospect of having to spend your whole life working in grease and dirt? Probably drowning in a sea of debt with a place this size and just couldn't face it any longer. Wrap it up. Let's not waste any more department money on lost causes."

"Yes sir."

He turned to look back at L.T. "If I were you, I wouldn't be interfering with an investigation. You're in enough trouble already."

"You call this an investigation?"

"Get him out of here," Mackenzie said, looking at Weaver.

L.T. walked back to his Explorer, then turned and spoke. "It's a suspicious death, Connie. Get a forensics team. It may be a homicide. Kendall told me he'd been threatened."

Mackenzie smiled and waved, then walked over and shook the hands of the two men in suits. L.T. noted that one looked a lot like the man who had deliberately pulled a car in front his, blocking his path and costing him a cup of coffee and a new cell phone. He got into his Explorer and drove in the direction of the police station.

Carla sat on the sofa in the drivers' lounge awaiting Marlin's call. Her steel-toed driving boots rested on the coffee table as she flipped through the latest Country Star Magazine. When she heard her name over the speaker, she leapt to her feet and hurried to the house phone.

"Hey," she said.

"Hey, Sis. Listen-"

"Where are you?" she interrupted.

"Just pulled into Ringgold, near the Tennessee Line. You're never gonna believe what just happened-."

She cut him off again. "Shut up and listen. They arrested a black guy for the murder of that trucker in Dade."

The line was silent.

"We're in the clear, Fish."

He still didn't answer.

"What did you want to tell me?" Carla asked.

"What? Nothing. Never mind, there are too many ears in this truckstop." Marlin was stunned by the news. He didn't think the police would know there had been a killing without first finding a body. And the body had gone into the gator-infested Withlacoochee River. "How could that happen?"

81

"I can't talk here, either. Where will you be tonight?"

"I feel like I can make the Windy today."

"All right, if you make Chicago, get a room and call me. In fact, call me whether you get that far or not. Get a room and call me. I'm going all the way to Cleveland today, I deliver at the Produce Market bright and early. Call me tonight at the Days Inn, junction of I-77 and I-480. You know the one, it's near Parma, got the Bob Evans across the street."

"Tell me one thing, Sis. Who the fuck died and made you president of my trucking company."

"Arnold Perkins." She hung up.

Ruby sat sipping a cup of stale coffee and smoking her third cigarette alone in an interview room at the White Falls Police Station. After an hour of making faces and once even flashing a breast at the surveillance camera up in the corner, the door opened and an officer walked in and said, "Shouldn't be much longer Ma'am. The Chief will be here shortly. He wants to question you himself."

"I want to call my lawyer."

The officer left the room without acknowledging her request. A few minutes later Chief Mackenzie entered and sat across from her with his hands on the table holding a few sheets of paper. "Thank you for coming in, Ruby. Are you okay? Do you need another cup of coffee? I'm sure it's not as good as what you serve at the diner."

She shook her head. "What did you bring me here for? And why wasn't I allowed to call my lawyer?"

"Lawyer? You don't need a lawyer; you're not under arrest. Not yet, anyway. I just need a few questions answered"

"Police come to my home, tell me I have to come down here with them, talk about using force and restraints and I'm not under arrest? What the hell do you do when you arrest someone? Shoot them?"

"I'm truly sorry about the misunderstanding, Ruby. I know you would never want to do anything but co-operate with this investigation. I'll make sure my officers know that."

"Will you please just tell me what I am doing here? I have a business to run and a dead brother to bury, you know."

The chief gave no indication that he was listening to her. He studied the papers in his hands a moment, and then spoke. "Ruby, have you ever been in trouble with the law before?"

"Before what?"

"Have you ever been in any trouble?"

"Yeah. My old man caught me in bed with his best friend. Like to killed me."

"I'm serious, Ruby."

"So was he."

"How's business at the diner?"

"I serve good food and the best coffee in town. I'm always busy."

"You must make a pretty good living."

"You don't get rich in a diner."

"You seem to be doing okay, though. In fact, according to your bank records, you seem to be doing very well." He looked at the papers again. "So well, in fact, that the manager of the White Falls Savings and

Loan thought it necessary to notify us of some unusual and suspicious activity in your accounts."

"What suspicious activity? Let me see that."

He showed her the mysterious large deposits that had occurred over the last several months. Her jaw dropped.

"I don't have that kind of money."

"We are aware of that. Question is, where did you get it? And what did you do with it?"

She shook her head. "I have no idea where that money came from or where it went. This is a mistake. The bank must have made a mistake."

"A bank makes a mistake and puts an extra forty grand in your account. No wait, let's see. They made three mistakes on the same account that amounted to forty thousand. Then they made another three mistakes by transferring those amounts to your personal account. Then what? They made another mistake that spent it?"

"I've never seen that much money."

"You're in a lot of trouble, Ruby. We know where money like this comes from. It's called proceeds of crime. Criminals know their dirty money can be traced back to them and link them to crimes. They need their money cleansed of any trace of crime so they launder it by passing it through legitimate businesses like your diner. We also know that it can't be done without the co-operation and assistance of the business owner, for a fee, of course."

Ruby slapped the table. "This is the craziest shit I've ever heard of. This is pure bullshit. I've never done any such thing and I don't have this money and you can't prove I did have it."

"Oh, yes we can, Ruby." He waved the papers at her. "We have your bank records and it's all in here. Now, why don't you make it easy on yourself and co-operate and tell us who you're fronting for."

"Are you going to arrest me?"

"Uh, not at this time, no. We're just beginning our investigation."

"Then I have nothing more to say to you."

Chief Mackenzie leaned back in his chair. An officer entered the room and said, "Chief, there's a call for you."

Mackenzie nodded and the young man left. "All right, Ruby. You can go now. But don't even think of leaving town."

The chief got up and walked to the door, then paused and said, "And Ruby, this is an official police investigation. If I were you, I would not breathe a word of it to anyone, especially your friend L.T. Stafford." He walked out and went directly to the next room where two men in suits were looking at the image of Ruby on a television monitor. One chuckled as Ruby flashed her middle finger at the camera then stomped out.

L.T. was waiting across the street in his Explorer when Ruby trudged out the front door of the police station. She climbed in next to him and said, "Fucking cops. No offence."

"Was it the money laundering matter?"

"Jesus, does everybody know about it, but me?"

"I told you about it yesterday. Don't you remember? That's why I punched Randy?"

"You did that for me? You lost your job and got your ass in trouble for me?"

"No, I did it for me. I've wanted to nail that asshole for at least twenty years. I finally figured out I wasn't getting any younger so I took the shot."

"L.T., you are just the sweetest man. You did it for me. Ahh."

"What did they say about me?"

"Can't tell you."

"Why not."

"Chief said not to."

"The Chief? The Chief was there while they questioned you?"

"More like, the Chief questioned me."

"Connie asked the questions? Who else was there? Fredericks? Patterson?"

"Nobody else. Just the Chief."

He shook his head. "The Chief questioned you himself? Did he ask about my involvement?"

"Nope. He just told me not to breathe a word to anyone, especially you."

"Now that does not make sense." He started the engine and drove away from the police station.

Chapter Eight

Orville Hennessey stood behind his desk, his back to the three men seated around it. He gazed out the rear window of the trailer-office of Hennessey Sand and Gravel. The September sun had slipped below the mounds of stone and sifted sand that marked the entrance to the gravel pit. Hennessey had made his first fortune in gravel decades earlier when his father died and left him a hundred and sixty acres of fine loam farmland. Determined never to work a farm again, he bought a truck, hired a man with a shovel and set about delivering loads of topsoil to new surveys in Toledo. By the time the soil was completely stripped he was already selling the gravel and sand layers to cement companies. When he hit limestone he sold mining rights to a quarry and made enough to buy the neighboring farm and start over.

Meanwhile, the leasing rock miners cut deep squares into the limestone bed of the first farm. When they finished, Orville found it a perfect place for the urban dwellers of Toledo to dispose of their garbage, for a fee, of course. Once the landfill reached capacity, Orville sold it to a developer along with a contract to provide and haul enough fill and topsoil for the development of White Falls' first eighteen-hole golf course.

After forty-eight years he was still in the sand and gravel business, but his real fortunes were accumulating elsewhere as one of the principals of PHD Holdings.

Without turning around he said, "How did it go with Ruby?"

"Oh, she's scared all right," said Conrad Mackenzie, Chief of White Falls Police Department. "But I think we should just let her be. She's too close to Stafford. If she gets him nosing around in her business, which would be our business, we could find ourselves in deep trouble."

Hennessey turned to face him and sat down. "Your job is to impress upon her the fact that no one, especially L.T. Stafford, knows anything about this. Can't you handle a little detail like that?"

"It's not always that easy, Orville. She and Stafford are in the sack together. In that kind of intimate relationship people share secrets."

"Intimate? L.T. Stafford? Jack Daniels is the only one old L.T.'s been intimate with in a long time."

"You know what I mean," said Mackenzie. "She lets slip a hint of her troubles, I can assure you he won't overlook it. That could be very dangerous for us."

"I agree," said Ned Dunphy, manager of White Falls Savings and Loan. He drummed his fingers on his bald head nervously. "May I remind you that this wasn't the usual setup? We only went after Ruby in the hope of getting L.T. off the White Falls Police Force. That's what the whole scenario was about." He chuckled and looked at Randall Pruitt. "It seems to have succeeded beyond our wildest dreams."

"Go ahead and laugh, you little weasel," said mayor Randall Pruitt, second husband of Orville's only daughter. "You weren't laughing while the sonofabitch was knocking my teeth out. You crapped your pants worrying you were going to be next. Seventeen hundred bucks worth of bridge work."

Dunphy's smirk receded.

"What's the revenue stream like at her diner?" asked Hennessey.

"Averages two thousand a day," said Dunphy.

Hennessey moved to his desk and punched some numbers into his calculator. "So, that's fifty grand a month times the usual twenty percent is ten thousand. Split four ways it equals twenty-five hundred a month each for as long as she owns and operates that greasy spoon. Everybody eats there. Hell, I eat there. I'm not about to pass up that kind of income just because you think this washed up booze hound, this ex White Falls policeman might be trouble. He's off the force, for Christ's sake. What harm can he possibly do us now?"

"Okay the money's good," said Mackenzie. "But hey, I know this guy. Yes, he's a boozer and he has problems. He's also a very thorough investigator. Once he gets a whiff of something offside he's like a dog with a bone. He just won't let go."

Hennessey turned and looked out the window again. "So, what you're telling me is that if L.T. Stafford is gone, we all get a raise in pay."

No one answered.

Wednesday morning Ruby padded up the back stairs to L.T.'s apartment just before seven. She knew she didn't need to wake him for work, but hoped he wouldn't mind a visit. After all that had happened she just wanted a few minutes with the one man who wouldn't give her any trouble. It wasn't bad enough she was grieving over the death of her brother, Arnold.

Now the cops were hassling her over something she has no idea about and just cannot be true. She plucked the key out of the bird feeder and let herself in. It surprised her that he was already dressed and poring over his pocket notebook, pencil in hand.

"What the hell is this?" asked Ruby. "I expect to see your naked ass this time of the morning."

"Couldn't sleep."

"Jesus, L.T. When's the last time you did?"

"Oh, I'm all right. I nodded off for a couple hours day before yesterday."

"Man, you have got to see a doctor about this."

"Hey, I do some of my best work in the middle of the night. I see a doctor; he'll give me a prescription for some pretty blue pills that will turn me into a zombie, night and day. I can do the same with a bottle of bourbon and still get to work in the morning."

"L.T., you don't work any more. You're officially retired. Take a deep breath and repeat after me, 'I am no longer gainfully employed. I will now spend more time relaxing with my friend Ruby and promise to dance the horizontal bop with her whenever her hormones are flying in formation'."

"That sheriff in…" he paused to look at his notes, "Dade City, Florida won't give me the time of day. I called to try to find out the details of Arnold's death. I identified myself as a police officer but not on official business. I told him I'm just a friend of the family and he promptly informed me that as a police officer I should be aware that no details of the case were to be released to the public until after next of kin had been notified. God I hate it when some hick lectures me on police procedure."

"You being a big city cop, and all."

He looked down his nose at her. "Then he proceeds to tell me that if I had said it was an official call I would have got a different answer. Fine. So, I play his game and tell him I'm making an official inquiry into the death of Arnold Perkins of Rutland Center, New York and he says, 'Go to hell' and the arrogant bastard hung up on me. You believe that shit?"

Ruby flopped next to him on the sofa. "I still can't believe it. Arnie's my big brother. He's always been there when I needed him. Now, I've got no one." Her eyes began to water.

L.T. slipped an arm around her shoulder and brought her close. She leaned her head against his chest. "Why won't they tell us anything?"

"Did you talk to Bertha?"

"They didn't tell her much of anything either, and she's his wife. All they said was that he had been found dead on the bank of the Whatyoumaycallit River and that he had been murdered. Course, that's Bertha. She wouldn't ask any questions anyway, except maybe who's going to harvest the corn now that her husband isn't coming home." She shook her head. "I've just got to know what happened to him. I just can't rest until I know there was some reason for all this to happen."

He squeezed her gently. "Then I better get started."

"Started what?"

"Packing. For Florida. I can't let you suffer like this. Besides, we both know I have time for a vacation in the Sunshine State now that I'm no longer gainfully employed."

"Ahh, L.T. You'd do that for me?"

"Naw, it's a vacation. I'm going down to find a nude beach where I can get everything suntanned." He kissed her and a tear ran down her cheek to wet their lips.

L.T. popped into the diner for a thermos of coffee. Ruby slipped two fried egg sandwiches into a bag and made him promise to eat them. He was out the door and in his six-year-old Ford Explorer by five past nine. The phone rang as she watched him drive away.

"Ruby's Diner," Priscilla answered. "It's for you, Rube. Ned Dunphy."

"Hello, Ned."

"Good morning, Ruby. I'm calling about the unusual activities in your account."

"Don't dance around it, Ned. Call me a criminal."

"It may not be as bad as all that."

"Oh really. Well I'm afraid the Chief of Police and his armed squads take a different view. They're talking about prison, Ned. And I've never seen a fucking red cent of this so-called laundered money. What do you make of that, Ned?"

"I'm afraid we have evidence to the contrary, Ruby. In fact, bank records show that approximately forty thousand dollars hit your business account in three deposits that were supposed to be your daily receipts."

"It's a crock of shit Ned. I've never had that much money in my entire life."

"Nevertheless, we have proof that that money was transferred to your personal account and withdrawn by you, shortly after being deposited. But listen, Ruby. Let's not debate this over the phone. I think I've come up with a way for you to avoid prison. Why don't you come down here when you finish your breakfast rush and we'll chat about my plan."

"You have an ass-saving plan?"

"Come to my office in an hour." He hung up.

Ruby couldn't wait an hour. She tossed her apron under the counter and told Priscilla she had to go to the Savings and Loan over a problem with her account. She immediately walked down the block and around the corner, still in uniform. She passed through the front door of the bank and strolled straight into the manager's office without knocking. Chief Mackenzie sat across from Dunphy. He cleared his throat and rose, but not to greet Ruby. He quickly stepped out, closing the door behind him.

"Uh, hey Ruby," said Ned, shuffling some papers on his desk and sliding them into a drawer. "Would you like some coffee?"

She just stared at him.

"Of course not. Have a seat."

She sat straight-backed, knees together and continued to stare.

"Yes," said Ned. "About that plan." He swiveled in his seat and reached for a file folder on the credenza behind his desk. "Chief Mackenzie has briefed me on the fact that he has provided the bank records for your inspection. Frankly, Ruby, he wants to prosecute you. He says minimum ten years prison for money laundering." He watched her jaw widen and her shoulders sag, let her suffer with the shock a moment, then spoke again. "Personally, I know you're a good person. We've never had a problem with you, I told him that."

Ruby wanted to rip off her pantyhose, wind them around the bald man's neck and tighten until his eyes popped. Instead, she said nothing. She had no idea where this money might be or who might have made these transactions but the deposit and withdrawal slips all appeared to bear her signature.

"I've talked to the chief on your behalf, Ruby. I think he's willing to listen to reason and accept that you are basically a good person who just got off the track a bit."

Ruby shook her head.

"Anyway, I believe if you are willing to accept the terms of this deal that he will consider dropping all charges."

"Look, Ned. I've checked my deposit and withdrawal slips for the dates you indicated and my copies don't look at all like the ones Chief Mackenzie showed me."

"Well, Ruby, we really wouldn't expect a money launderer to keep damning evidence would we?"

She slumped in the chair as depression began to smother her.

"The chief said if you are willing to make restitution he will consider it a mistake and drop the charges, since no one gets hurt in that case."

"No one except Ruby," she mumbled under her breath. "Ned," she raised her voice. "You're not listening to me. I've never had that kind of money and I don't have it now. I can't pay it back."

"Yes you can, Ruby. Calm down and listen to me. First, because we know you are a woman of high moral...uh, high standards... Because I know you are mainly dependable I have arranged for a private lender to cover your debt with the Savings and Loan."

"How the hell could I ever pay it back?"

"Here's how. You agree to a partnership agreement with the lender, PHD Holdings. From then on, PHD will share in your daily revenue. Namely, you agree to allow the Savings and Loan to withhold twenty percent of gross revenue to be forwarded to PHD. Because you are willing to provide them with a partnership, PHD forgives the loan. So, you don't even have to pay it back. We just see to it that PHD gets their share of the gross on a daily basis. And of course, this is a silent partnership. You still run the diner yourself."

"Jesus, Ned. Only twenty percent of gross. Just what the fuck am I supposed to live on? If I had an extra twenty percent don't you think you would have seen some accumulation in my account? I'm never more than a day ahead of starvation now. You or this PHD takes a slice off the top of that, I might as well join Kendall Griffith."

"Would you rather go to prison?"

She sank lower in her seat.

"Under the terms of this partnership agreement, if you are unable or unwilling to remain in business your assets may be foreclosed upon by the lender. That includes your personal assets."

"What about blood? Would the bastards want my blood just in case my assets aren't adequate?"

"Ruby, I really think you should be grateful. PHD has made a very generous offer of bailing out a business woman in trouble."

"Well, thank you PHD. Thanks for ramming it so far up my ass I feel like I'm choking. Anything else?"

"Yes. As a final condition you must tell no one of this agreement."

"Who, in her right mind, would want to brag about a screwing like this? My lips are sealed. That's unusual for me."

"You agree then?"

"Let me guess. You have the paperwork all ready for me to sign."

Chapter Nine

L.T. cruised south on I-75 nearing Lexington, Kentucky at one o'clock in the afternoon. He had been studying tractor-trailer rigs all the way down, weaving around them, driving beside them, trying to match up the photograph of Gary Turner's missing truck. He was pretty certain its appearance would have been altered by now. It probably would no longer bear the name of New York Truck Brokers, might even be painted a different color. L.T. felt somewhat overwhelmed. All the rigs looked pretty much the same to him, save subtle differences.

The OIL light on the instrument panel switched on and remained lit. His eyes scanned the highway ahead for a sign of an exit. The engine began to clatter as he took the next off-ramp and swung the vehicle into a truck stop. He shut the engine down and coasted toward the repair shop to avoid any further damage to the vehicle. By the time he propped the hood open, a mechanic stood beside him wiping his greasy hands on an even greasier rag.

"Y'all got trouble, mister?"

"OIL light came on. Then the engine started this rattling, tapping noise. Do you think it's serious?"

He pulled the dipstick, turned to spit tobacco juice on the hot asphalt, and then studied the oil level indicator. "Yep," he said and spat again.

"What do you think it is?"

"One of two things."

"You know that already, just by checking the oil?"

"Nope. You asked what I think, not what I know. What I know is you have lots of oil in this engine." He waved the dipstick in front of L.T. for him to see. "But it sounds like you have low or no oil pressure. So, that makes me think it's either a busted oil pump or a spun bearing. If it's the oil pump, we can fix it in a few days. If it's a bearing, well, you're pretty much fucked." He spat for emphasis.

"Any place around here I can get it fixed quicker?"

"Nope. Where you headed?"

"Florida."

"Go on in and tell Mavis at the fuel desk. Then go and eat lunch in the restaurant. I reckon by the time you get to dessert, Mavis will have you a ride to Florida. Don't worry about your truck. I'll get it fixed up for you."

"How much will it cost to fix it?"

"If it's the oil pump, a couple or three hundred. If it's a spun bearing, a whole lot more."

L.T. left the number of his cell phone and headed inside to look for Mavis and have lunch. He was finished eating and on his second cup of coffee when he heard his name on the speaker system. He left a ten on the table and went to see the chunky woman at the fuel desk. She stood chatting with a man about thirty-five years old, dressed in jeans and tee shirt and leaning on the counter.

"Mr. Stafford," said Mavis. "This here's Diesel Doobie. Doobie, Mister Stafford is the gentleman who needs to get to Florida."

The two shook hands. "Did she say Diesel Doobie?" asked L.T.

"Named after two of my worst habits. Mavis here could tell you about my best traits, though."

The large woman blushed and turned away.

"Are you going to Florida?" L.T. asked.

"As we speak. You ever drive a truck before?"

"No, never."

"Nothing to it. Like sex. You're nervous about it the first time. After that, you just drive it home."

"Don't you need a special license for that?"

"Don't worry about it, eh. I'll lend you mine. I'm a day late, dog tired and need to get to Cigar City." The man took a few steps toward the door, turned and looked back. "Better grab your luggage, Mr. Stafford. We're going to the Bikini State."

L.T. followed him out the door. The man waited while he jogged to his disabled Explorer and retrieved a thermos and a small, black suitcase. They crossed the parking lot together and stopped next to a silver-gray Freightliner with a flatbed trailer. The trailer was stacked high with what looked like new steel frames of vehicles all painted black.

"You can stow your stuff in the sleeper," the driver said, unlocking the passenger door.

L.T. hoisted himself up and in. He had pulled over a few of these big rigs for traffic violations but had never seen the inside of one. He was impressed at the amount of space inside the cab and its connecting sleeper compartment. He pushed his suitcase under the bunk and settled into the passenger seat as Diesel Doobie slid in behind the oversize steering wheel. A turn of the key and the big rig shuddered and clattered to life.

"The first thing you need to know," said Doobie," is that the only time you shove the clutch all the way to the floor is when the rig is standing still. There's a clutch brake on the mainshaft of the transmission that engages when you depress the pedal all the way. It stops the mainshaft from spinning long enough to slip the transmission into gear. But if you shove that clutch down all the way when the truck is rolling, the mainshaft can't stop because the rear wheels are driving it. It shears the key off the brake and makes it very difficult to get the truck in gear when you're stopped. And if there's one thing I hate it's sitting at a stoplight grinding the gears. I hate looking like a rookie. Watch me."

His left foot depressed the clutch pedal all the way to the floor. He waited a few seconds, and then eased the gear stick forward until he felt the spring-loaded detent catch and hold the stick in place. "Now, what you have to do to get it rolling is begin to ease up on your left foot while your pushing down lightly on the fuel pedal with your right." As he demonstrated, the rig gently rolled forward very smoothly, L.T. noted. "You've got to think of her like a woman, like Dolly Parton, eh. To get her going you have to massage one tit one way, one tit the other way at the same time without making her say ouch."

L.T. was thinking he couldn't be serious about wanting him to drive, but Doobie continued.

"You have thirteen forward speeds but you'll only use twelve. First gear is a real bull low. You only need it if you're pulling out of one of those three-day potholes in the Wolverine State."

"Three-day potholes?"

"The roads are so bad in Michigan if you drive into a pothole it can take you three days just to find your way out."

"Say, you're not serious about me driving this freight train?"

Doobie looked at him with mouth half open a moment, then continued. "So you start in second gear and from there it's just a regular H pattern like a four-on-the-floor. This little button on the side of the shift knob has three positions: low, medium, and high. You make sure it's in low when you start off, you run through the first four, then shift into mid range, move the stick back to the start position and go through the next four. Then you move the little range selector to high, start the stick over again and by the time you hit the last hole we're flying. Can you remember all that?"

"You're kidding, right?" This is a joke."

"Don't worry about it, eh. I'll coach you through it at first. You know, it's really simple once you get the hang of it. But I remember when I was just learning; one of the toughest things was to recall what gear you're in so you know where to go next. Watch me." Traffic cleared and Doobie eased the truck out onto the highway, shifting gears in rapid succession as he worked through the lower ranges. He swung a right onto the southbound ramp of I-75 and in a matter of minutes they were at cruising speed, running with the traffic. The lesson continued.

"Just remember to watch the tachometer. At eighteen hundred RPMs you shift to a higher gear. These hills will give you some trouble. When you find you're foot is flat on the floor but you're still losing speed going up a hill, you know you're going to need to grab a lower gear. When the needle drops to fifteen hundred you shift to the next lower gear. Don't look at me like you have no idea what's going on here. I'm a good teacher. I've taught women to drive. The only difference between them and you is that they put out. Now pay attention because my body is running out of gas. You'll be taking over soon."

"I thought all you truckers did drugs to keep you awake."

"Pocket rockets," Doobie said. "Yeah, but you can only run so long on them until you find out you just can't go no more, eh. Like that truck of yours. Tank full of gas but no oil and you can't drive it another mile. My wife hates it when I come home all limp-dick like that. I get home from a six or eight-day run she expects me to perform circus acts over her naked body."

"Where's your home, Doobie?"

"Toronto, home of the Maple Leafs."

"Ah, that explains why you talk so funny."

"Yeah, eh."

A little after four they pulled into the welcome center at the Tennessee State Line. Doobie left the engine running as the two men headed for the rest room. Doobie was still jabbering away with insights into how to drive an eighteen-wheeler. L.T. did his best to follow. When they returned to the truck, Doobie told him to take the driver seat.

L.T. managed to get the truck rolling with a mild lurch. Doobie was in the passenger seat talking him through it.

"Remember to double-clutch like I showed you. Only half-way down with the clutch now, you're rolling."

L.T. wheeled the big rig out of the parking area and onto the ramp. "Jesus, it's power steering. I thought all you guys had to have ape arms to muscle these things around." He was feeling good about himself now, smiling as he drove the monster truck.

"Left turn signal, got to merge into traffic. Keep working the speed up as we head into the grade. This is Jellico. This is the longest, steepest hill on I-75. The toughest place to learn to drive. You master this, the rest is downhill, so to speak."

The smile left L.T.'s face. He fumbled with the range selector, trying to move it from low to medium while shifting the lever back to the start position. The truck showed no mercy. It lost speed rapidly on the upgrade and by the time L.T. sorted out the controls he was in too high a gear to pull the truck. The diesel engine coughed and shuddered and the truck continued to slow. A driver in a tanker blasted his air horn.

"Throw on the right turn signal and move onto the shoulder. Hold the clutch halfway down until we stop. That's it. Now feather the brakes."

L.T. managed to ease the rig to a stop on the side of the road. "Okay," he said, "I think I've had enough. You can take over now."

Doobie chuckled. "Don't worry about it, eh. Dolly forgives you. Let me give you a little tip about using the range selector. Before you start to shift, move the range selector to medium while your foot is still on the accelerator. She won't up shift until the weight is off when you hit neutral. It'll make it like the automatic transmission in that Explorer of yours. Okay, maybe not, but it'll be a hell of a lot easier."

When the traffic cleared, L.T. tried the hill again. This time, with Doobie's coaching, he rolled the truck smoothly up the mountain toward Knoxville. Doobie slipped back into the sleeper. After a moment, the aroma of burning leaves of the cannabis variety made it necessary for L.T. to crack the window.

"Just keep it on I-75. I'll be comatose for a while." Doobie's voice was squeaky as he spoke without breathing to hold in the smoke. "Do like I showed you at the scale house. And remember to feather the brakes. It's air pressure, like stepping on a tennis ball." After that, the only sounds were the drone of the diesel, the whine of the tires, and the occasional crackly voice on the CB radio. L.T. settled into a groove and just drove.

Chapter Ten

The sun sank low outside the passenger window as L.T. wheeled the big rig to a stop at the Georgia welcome center. He had a little trouble judging the turn into the angled truck parking space and finished up covering two spots. With few trucks parked at that time of day there remained lots of room for others so, he was satisfied with his effort. L.T.'s hands were clammy with sweat and cramping up from being clamped tightly about the Freightliner's steering wheel. Doobie rose to a sitting position on the berth, awakened by the sudden lack of motion.

"Peach State, eh." It took him a minute to focus on his wristwatch. "Just after seven. Three hours, not bad. Course, I'd have done it in two and a half. But you're a rookie, eh. That's fine. Want to keep going?"

"No, I think I've had enough for my first solo. It'll be dark soon. I don't know if I'm ready for driving under those conditions. Besides, I'm ready for a break."

The two men stretched their legs, and then motored on.

"Where you from, Stafford?"

"Ohio. White Falls. It's a small town -."

"Thirty-seven miles east of T-Town."

"You know it?"

"Nice little diner, there, eh. Cute chick running the place. Good food. Nice ass."

L.T. grinned. "You have been there. Ruby Treatt's a friend of mine. I live in the apartment upstairs, she's my landlady."

"Ruby, yeah, that's her. I stopped in there once a couple years back. I recall I was running from Cleveland to Toledo but had to stay off the Ohio Turnpike since I was a bit over the legal weight limit. So, I'm bee-bopping along Route 20 when a dude going the other way tells me the PUCO boys are checking trucks just outside Fremont. Had to wait them out at the diner in White Falls. Nice little town. Sweet ass, that Ruby."

"That's amazing, you remembering that."

"Naw, I been everywhere, eh. Wife says I have a pornographic memory. Point is, I never forget an ass like that. So, what do you do in the hustle and bustle of White Falls, Stafford?"

"Call me L.T. Up until a few days ago I could have arrested you for that little number you were smoking in the Smokeys."

Doobie's jaw dropped. "No shit. You're a cop? I ain't got no more, I swear. You on vacation or what?"

"Permanent."

"You quit?"

"Retired is what they're officially calling it."

"What are you calling it?"

"Aw, they fired my ass. They've been trying to for years."

"What'd you do? This ain't one of those sexual harassment things, is it?"

"Something way more pleasant than that. I sucker-punched the mayor."

"No shit, eh." He chuckled. "Why?"

"It's a long story."

"Ain't they all, officer? Ain't they all? So, you are going to vacation in Florida?"

"Not exactly. Ruby's brother was driving a truck down there. Turned up dead near Dade City this morning. Ruby's been good to me when no one else cared. I owe it to her to find out what happened to him."

"Shit," said Doobie, and didn't say anything more.

Carla lay back on the motel bed, sipping a Busch and watching Country Music videos on cable. She was clad only in panties. She always carried a nightie but almost never wore it. Some nights she even shed the panties. She kept the music just loud enough so that she could still make out the hum of the diesel refrigeration unit on the Great Dane trailer parked across the asphalt lot at the Days Inn near Parma, Ohio just outside Cleveland. It was a little past nine-thirty Tuesday evening. She would grab a few hours sleep, rise at three a.m. and make the short run to the Cleveland Produce Market to offload the grapefruit. By five-thirty she'd be back in bed at the motel and would sleep until noon. Her load home wouldn't be ready for pickup until Thursday morning in Toledo. This week's work was half over and it felt good to know she would have the day off tomorrow.

The telephone startled her. She had forgotten Marlin would be calling.

"Hey, Fish."

"Hey, Sis."

"You make the Windy?"

"Hell yes. I'm on the north side of Chicago. Just a hop, skip and jump to Oshkosh tomorrow. Load popping corn outside of Evansville, Indiana Thursday morning for the Port of Tampa. I'll be home late Friday night."

"So, what's so important you were dying to tell me?"

"Carla, you should have seen this asshole. I'm trucking along north of Marietta, minding my own business. This major jerk in a Beemer blows his horn at me, cuts me off, shoots me the bird."

"And like that's a big deal?"

"Will you shut up and listen to me. I tail the guy to a gas station. While he's inside paying I meander past his car and slice the valve stem on the right rear. He gets back on the Interstate. Ten miles down the road, there he is. Got the ass end up on the jack, he's out there with the wheel off. I pull over and make like I'm going to help him."

"Didn't he know you were the one he fingered?"

"Naw, trucks all look alike to these suit and tie executives. I park behind him, walk over and accidentally on purpose kick the lug nuts under the car. So he's screaming at me, calling me shit-for-brains and all. I get back in my truck, he rants and raves five minutes or so, finally off comes the shirt and tie. Next thing I know he's under the car on his belly. I ram the Beemer and it's off the jack. Scratch one aggressive driver with · the overactive finger. Teach that motherfucker not to mess with me."

"Wow," she said without emotion.

"Wow? Fucking wow? That's all you got to say?"

"What the fuck is this all about, Fish? You wake up with a hangover so the first guy that gets out of line gets dead? We need this? What?"

"Hey, Carla, you started it. You kill this trucker and all of a sudden you think you run my trucking business. You're Queen Shit."

"Our trucking business."

"Yeah, well not anymore. I just evened up the score." His voice picked up volume. "I run this company, not you. Don't you forget it."

"Yeah, whatever." She slipped her free hand inside the waistband of her panties and scratched lightly at the bush. "Sometimes Fish it's like your brain just takes a vacation, you know. You're out there somewhere, we can see you, but we have no idea where you're at or where you're going. You killed this guy for no reason at all. Do the words 'death by lethal injection' mean anything at all to you? You're just bound to get us caught, aren't you, Fish? I killed to save you from a crazy Yankee trucker with a gun on you. You killed this guy for no reason. No reason whatever."

"Wrong. Totally wrong. I did this guy to get you under control."

"Under control? You think you can control me, Fish? You want that assignment? I'll show you control and I won't get us into prison or dead doing it. You talk about me being on overload. Look at you. Your brain is going four hundred miles an hour and you can't stop it. That's overload, brother."

"Fuck you, Carla."

"Don't you hang up on me, you sonofabitch. Listen. That black dude on the Harley – the one that showed up at the ranch Saturday - followed me yesterday. I pulls out of Wheatley's packing house, there he is across the road. Tails me all the way to

Brunswick. Comes in the truck stop and tells me how he found the body-."

"How the hell could he find the body? It was midnight, we put the guy in the river."

"This guy fishes under the bridge at night. The stiff got tangled in his lines."

"Bullshit."

"Bullshit nothing. He showed me the guy's wallet. It was definitely the same guy. Said he fished your screwdriver out of the dude's back and knows you did it. He figured that was his ticket to becoming a partner in an interstate trucking company."

"Jesus."

"Yeah, glad to see I've finally got your attention."

"Hey, you killed him, not me. But you said this morning the black biker was charged with murder."

"That's right, big brother. Little sister saved your ass not once, but twice. Can I get a little respect now?"

"Oh, right. I'm supposed to believe you had the jig arrested?"

"I let him believe that he had you cold. I took him out and showed him his new truck and you know what? I had him by the balls by then. I sweet-talked him into going and putting the body back in the river so the gators could get rid of the evidence. And when I saw him heading back south, I just let the State Troopers in on what I had overheard a black biker say at a truck stop, how he had killed a white trucker near Dade City, left his body on the bank of the Withlacoochee near the US98 Bridge."

"You went to the cops? Are you spun?"

"No, you are. I swear, your brain is definitely on overload. I called them. I used a phony name. They have no idea who reported it. The point is they caught the guy. He had the dead man's wallet; he had the murder weapon in his saddlebag. It don't matter what he tells them about us, they've got so much evidence on him he's toast."

"This doesn't change a thing, Carla."

"Damn straight, it does. She hung up on him, then called the switchboard and told them not to put any more calls through. She leaned back on the bed, turned the music up and teased at the hairs between her legs.

Doobie and L.T. had stopped for a late supper at the truck stop next to the Atlanta Farmer's Market in Forest Park, Georgia. After their meal Doobie showed his student how to perform a walk-around inspection with a mental checklist, examining the rig under the bright lights of the truck stop. They thumped tires to check for flats, looked for separating treads; they eyed the lug nuts on all the disc wheels looking for any sign of rust that would indicate a cracked wheel stud or loose wheel nut. They tugged at all chains securing the load to ensure they were tight, then finished off by checking the lights and the trailer air and electrical connections.

Shortly after ten Tuesday evening they were rolling south again on I-75, leaving the lights of Atlanta in the rearview mirrors. The red-orange glow of the truck's marker lights softly illuminated the interior of the truck cab. Similar lights from an endless stream of trucks had a hypnotic effect on L.T. and he found himself repeatedly dozing and waking with the jostling of the heavy truck's air-ride seat. Doobie had grown unusually quiet at the wheel and L.T. found himself enjoying the break in his driving instruction. The constant chatter from the CB almost blended with the drone of the engine and the whine of tires to make it more and more difficult for L.T. to stay awake. Then an argument broke out between two drivers on the CB and soon racial slurs were flying over the airwaves. L.T. was jolted wide-eyed by the harsh language. Other drivers broke in and the arguing became intense.

He looked at Doobie who seemed totally nonplussed by the commotion. "Are these guys going to kill each other or what?" L.T. asked.

Doobie smiled. "Naw, let them be. Nobody will get hurt. It's good for them, eh."

"Good for them?"

"As an officer of the law you must know that most truck wrecks – and the most deadly wrecks - occur during the hours between midnight and six in the morning. You can see for yourself there are a lot of men working out here tonight. It's a typical night. And we're all fighting internal clocks that make us think we should be asleep by eleven, eh. So, drivers will do whatever they need to do to stay awake, to stay safe, to stay alive. Some argue. Some sing. Some talk to an imaginary passenger. Whatever it takes."

"What do you do?"

"Me? Sometimes I start up a conversation with another driver I've never met before. Lots of guys do that, eh. But if I'm really fighting sleep, I tell stories."

"Stories?"

"Yeah, I just make shit up, eh. Listen."

They listened to the numerous conversations being carried over the short-range airwaves. When a sleepy voice asked if anyone had any pocket rockets, Doobie grabbed the microphone and keyed it. "Driver, you don't want to be doing no pocket rockets. Them pills are very bad for your health. Trust me, I had an awful experience recently with pocket rockets."

There was silence for a moment, and then another voice broke in and asked, "What happened, driver?"

"Whew," Doobie said into the microphone. "For a minute there I thought no one would ask. Well, it happened last winter. You see, my wife loves me dearly so she sometimes puts a pocket rocket in my pocket so I make it home to her quicker and perform all those circus acts over her naked body."

Another voice cut in and said, "Driver, I know your wife. She told me she does that to get you the hell down the road."

"Hah," said Doobie. "Shut up and let me tell it." He grinned at L.T. who was watching and listening intently. "So, this one time I stop off in the Motor City to see my girlfriend and I forget there's a pocket rocket in my pocket. She gets rubbing her naked self all over me and she's so hot that my pocket rocket goes off in my pocket and it blows all the feathers off my chicken, eh. Wouldn't you know it, my chicken catches cold, starts coughing and sneezing and spits right in her eye. She finally saves my chicken by wrapping a fur collar around it to keep it warm. What do you make of all that?"

Another voice cut in, saying, "Yeah, that sounds like you. Your wife told me that premature ejaculation was the only way you could deliver a load early."

L.T. nearly pissed himself.

After a time Doobie grew quiet again, listening to the crackling voices on the CB and studying the road ahead. His hands massaged the steering wheel continuously, making the required adjustments that kept all eighteen wheels in line. His eyes would move in never-ending cycles from the windshield to the mirrors to the instruments and back to the windshield, always scanning. In the diesel droning darkness L.T. could no longer avoid thinking of the loss he suffered in the death of Kendall Griffith. They had known each other forever, and yet, L.T. surmised that if he had really known this man he should have recognized that he was in need of help. This is what friends do. They help you through the difficult times so you don't end up killing yourself, he thought, and for the first time in days craved a drink.

He should be back in White Falls for he was certain to miss his friend's funeral service while off to Florida. He should be there to console Edie. She would expect him to be there. Everyone would expect him to be there. He should be there to find out what caused his friend to die. If it really was suicide, what drove him to it? If it wasn't, then who killed him and why? He should be there and he knew it. He would be conspicuous in his absence and that would give the folks of White Falls one more reason to withhold respect for him. He wanted a drink.

L.T. made up his mind that when he returned to White Falls he would do whatever it took to find out what or who was responsible for the death of his friend. This time he would keep digging, keep investigating, keep searching until he found the answer. He would not let the truth die with his friend as he had when Willard Paetz died. He would start by finding out who were the two men in suits that had been hanging around, the men that Kendall had called business consultants. He also wanted to know if Kendall had any partners, silent or otherwise. But those issues would have to wait until he returned to White Falls. Ruby was also a good friend and right now she needed him to find out why her brother had died. Ruby first, for now, anyway.

He knew there was no way Ruby could have been laundering money. In the first place, she didn't make enough to have deposited an extra forty thousand over the summer. And he believed her when she said she had no knowledge of that money or where it went. But who else would have access to her business account? Priscilla? Perhaps, but only for making deposits in Ruby's absence. She wouldn't be able to transfer the money to Ruby's personal account and then withdraw it. Was Ruby's signature on the deposit slips? He couldn't recall, having only taken a quick glimpse at the evidence during the meeting with the chief, the mayor, and the banker. White Falls being a small town, everyone in that bank knows Ruby. It wouldn't matter if someone tried to forge Ruby's signature. No one in the bank would allow it. Unless, he surmised, it was an inside job.

What if one of the tellers had money problems, or a gambling addiction, or even compulsive spending habits? What about that Claire Mackie? She was always dressed like she was yacht club material but her husband was such a dweeb, a real quiet guy who worked as a mechanic for Kendall Griffith. That woman had to be spending more than the two of them were making. Where was the money coming from? Was she diverting it from other client accounts? Embezzling? Or was she actually passing dirty money through business accounts to launder it for someone and getting paid off for doing it? Someone like Kendall Griffith's new business consultants maybe? Was Kendall having similar problems? Were they the partners Kendall said were threatening him?

At noon Wednesday L.T. stood on a corner in Dade City reading a story in the weekly newspaper about the capture of local resident Elvis Wood, alleged killer of Arnold Perkins of Rutland Center, New York. Wood occupied a cell at the Pasco County Jail, just down the street. L.T. walked in that direction. He entered the County building and was directed by the receptionist to the lockup area. A uniformed guard greeted him at the entrance to the secure area.

"Good afternoon, sir. Can I help you?"

"I understand you are holding Elvis Wood here?"

"What is the nature of your inquiry, sir?"

"I'm family, I want to visit him." What the hell, nothing else had worked with these people.

The guard smiled. "I'm sorry, sir. But I just can't see any family resemblance between you and the inmate. Care to try again?"

"I'd like to talk to him."

"Sorry. That privilege is reserved for his attorney. Sheriff Henry says absolutely no visitors."

"Any idea where I might find his attorney?"

"I'd say start with the Public Defender's office. Good day, sir."

L.T. made his way around to the Office of the Public Defender. A pretty blonde woman in her late thirties smiled up at him from the desk inside the entrance.

"Hi, I'm looking for the person who will be representing Elvis Wood."

"And what is your interest in Mr. Wood and his defense counsel?"

Jesus, he thought, everybody's in the interrogation business. "I'm a friend of the family of the deceased. I'm down here to try to shed some light on what events resulted in the death of my friend's brother."

"Well, I'm sure all of the details will come to light during the trial."

L.T. rolled his eyes. "I really don't think it's necessary to make the victim's family wait that long to find out what happened. Do you?"

"Look sir, I'm afraid there's really no way we can help you right now."

"Ma'am, how would you like to be a grieving sister who wants to know what killed her brother and not be able to get any information at all?" He was getting seriously annoyed.

"Why don't you try Sheriff Henry? I'm sure he can help you. He's in charge of the homicide investigation."

"I'm afraid Sheriff Henry is even more of a control freak than you, lady."

She gave a slight smile, not offended by his comment. "Look, Mr.…What did you say your name was?"

"I didn't, but it's Stafford. L.T. Stafford from White Falls, Ohio."

"Look, Mr. Stafford. I understand you've come a long way from up yonder. But I'm sure you can appreciate that when defense counsel is preparing a case for what is certain to be a murder trial, we really don't have the inclination or the time to be dealing with vindictive relatives of the deceased. I really feel that it is in our mutual interests for you to get your information elsewhere. But for your information, Elvis Wood will be defended by Ray White."

"Thank you, ma'am. Can you tell me where I might find Mr. White?"

The smiling blonde woman extended a hand. "Hey, Mr. Stafford. I'm Raylene White."

He shook her hand and smiled back. "I'm sorry, Miss White. It's been hell week for me. First Mr. Perkins is missing, and then he turns up dead. I lost my job. My car broke down and I had to leave it in Kentucky and hitch a ride with a trucker. Hell week, I tell you."

"Lost your job, huh? I'm sorry. What kind of work do you do?"

"I'm a – that is, I was a police officer."

Her eyes widened. "How does a police officer lose his job? Never mind, I don't think I want to know."

"Oh, I just punched somebody."

"And they suspended you for that?"

"No ma'am, they fired my ass."

"The nerve. Who did you strike, the mayor?"

"You're extremely intuitive, aren't you?"

She laughed. "Are you serious? You punched the mayor? What did your family think of that? Your wife?"

"Tell me, Miss White, do you know why this Elvis Wood killed my friend's brother?"

"Why Mr. Stafford. You, a former police officer assuming a suspect is guilty before being tried. I thought you cops were supposed to be objective."

"How about you, Miss White. Do you think he's guilty or innocent?"

"Doesn't matter what I think. What's important is that justice be served. Still, I wish I could get the sheriff to be a little more objective. Unfortunately, he has so much damning evidence against my client I'm afraid we don't stand a chance of acquittal. My client has offered an explanation of how the evidence came into his possession. But the sheriff won't follow up on it. He figures he's got a nice, clean case and the District Attorney seems to subscribe to that sentiment also. They don't want to muddy the waters, even if it's with the truth. Wish I could find just one objective investigator to run down a few leads for me. Say, how long did you say you're in town, Mr. Stafford?

"I'm not sure."

"You have years of investigative experience, I'll bet."

"I don't think I like what you're driving at, Miss White."

"Call me Ray. Suppose I let you talk to my client. Would you promise not to attempt to inflict bodily harm upon him? And would you further agree to checking into the validity of his story?"

"Miss White. Ray. I don't really care much about your client. But I do want to get to the bottom of what happened to Mr. Perkins." He rolled his eyes again and looked up at the crown molding around the ceiling. "I can't believe I'm doing this."

She snatched up the phone. "I'll get us in to see him this afternoon. Why don't you have a look at his file." She passed it to him.

Chapter Eleven

Carla slept through until three in the afternoon. She slipped into her jeans and walked across the street to the Bob Evans restaurant for some blueberry pancakes but was pissed at the fact that they don't serve grits after eleven a.m. When she got back to her room she showered, brushed her teeth and slipped into fresh panties and a short, red dress. A taxi arrived and took her to Nashville Road, a popular Country Music bar talked up by drivers throughout the Midwest. It was too early for any live entertainment, but the jukebox was playing steadily and a few drivers, mostly men, were already hanging around the bar. She slid onto a barstool and slowly crossed her long legs. Even in the dimly lit bar the creamy flesh contrasted coolly with the hot red dress. Before she could order, the bartender slid a bourbon on the rocks in front of her and pointed over his left shoulder. A short, chubby driver in a Roadway Freight uniform smiled and raised his glass. She slid the drink back at the bartender and asked for a beer. The smile disappeared from the trucker's face. He picked up his drink and stumbled around the bar toward her.

"What's the matter? Don't you think I'm sexy enough for you?" He was wobbling as he walked and talked. "For all you know, I could have a foot long weenie so don't judge a book by it's cover. I'll give you a ride on the baloney pony you'll never forget."

The drunken driver suddenly stumbled over the outstretched leg of a clean-cut young man with rugged features and a Stetson seated at a table alone. The man on the floor tried to get up but was met with a single quick jab from the cowboy and slid back down to the floor. The bartender picked up the phone and moments later two men appeared and dragged the driver across the dance floor and out the back door. The cowboy smiled at Carla and touched a finger to the brim of his hat with a nod in her direction. She turned in her seat and faced forward, ignoring him.

A moment later, a Stetson dropped onto the bar next to her and the handsome stranger leaned over it.

"Can I buy you a drink, ma'am?"

"I already have one," she replied with a slight smile as the bartender set down her beer. She picked it up and sipped at it.

"I suppose you're thinking I should thank you for rescuing me from that drunken old fart. Well, I'll have you know I can take care of myself."

The stranger was still smiling. "Take a look around you, beautiful. See anyone you'd like to spend time with?"

She glanced about the room, eyes darting from one to another and another. There were a half-dozen other men sitting around drinking, belching, and scratching their balls. Two were fat, another was ugly as a flat tire, and the rest just were not clean.

"Life is short, Angel. I'm at the table over there if you decide you'd like to cut the crap and have a good time." He smiled, slipped his hat onto his head and returned to his table. Carla picked up her beer and followed.

"Okay, so you're cute. Did you have to humiliate my ass in front of these people?"

"First, your ass is so fine no one would ever consider it humble. Second, in front of what people? These are zombies. Like dead Indians. You and me, we're the only people in here."

She broke into a grin. He'd scored a few more points.

L.T. jotted notes continuously as Elvis spoke. He let the black man tell his story in its entirety before reviewing his notes to ask questions. He liked to get the big picture first without getting sidetracked by details. Then he would work through and key in on the individual points. It was a fundamental way of catching a bad liar. If the questioning led to obvious conflicts, the person was lying.

"Tell me how to find this ranch."

Elvis directed him through Zephyrhills then said, "You can't see it from the road. Can't even tell it's there."

"How did you find it, then?"

"Oh, it was tricky, all right. See, I tailed this truck and van from the bridge, must've been after midnight. So, I knew about where it was. But by the time I pulled up, their lights had disappeared. I had trouble finding it the next day 'cause there ain't nothing to mark the lane. Got to watch for the grove of live oaks with the dirt laneway that disappears into them. Looks like it goes nowhere. But that ranch is back there beyond the trees. One minute you're in a dark jungle of oaks and hanging moss, next minute you're parked in front of the house and barn in full sunlight."

"What do you remember about the ranch?"

"Not much to tell, really. Not much of a ranch. Looked like they must've raised beef there at some time. I crossed a cattle gap on the way in."

"Cattle gap?"

"It's to stop cattle from wandering out your laneway when you don't have a gate. See, what they do is they dig down the full width of the lane about a foot or so deep and then they criss-cross these two-by twelve's on their edges a foot apart so that cars – or trucks – can pass into and out of the place with no trouble. But if a cow tries to get out he finds himself standing in holes and can't make it across. Most of the ranches around here use them so they don't have to open and close the gate whenever they want to go somewhere. See, as a rule people tend to be lazy around here. Funny thing, though, I didn't see a single cow there."

"Was there a barn? Maybe the cows were inside."

"Naw. Only thing in the barn was a tractor-trailer rig. I saw the back doors of a Great Dane trailer, saw the name on the back door. Big shiny motherfucker.

"If you didn't kill this man, why were you in possession of his wallet and the murder weapon when you were picked up?"

"Simple. Leverage. I needed them to buy my way into the trucking business. Mr. Stafford, I never had a real job in my life. Sure, I've off-loaded trucks over at the Winn-Dixie warehouse in Tampa for a few bucks here and there. I've worked in fruit packinghouses for a season. Hell, I've even wiped down cars in a detail shop. Hah. Detail shop they called it. Wasn't nothing but a car wash. Now, I ride a broken down old hog made up mostly from stolen parts, I live in an old trailer with whatever old queen I can get to do my laundry for a time, and I make enough to keep gas in the scooter and beer on the table by catching a few mullet and catfish and selling them to the soul food restaurants. It ain't a living. My biggest dream is to drive a shiny new eighteen-wheeler, that Great Dane trailer all polished up and sparkling 'til you could see yourself in it. People would respect me, man. I'd be somebody. Know what I mean?"

"Maybe you're dream was big enough and close enough to kill for."

"If you believe that, then tell me, where's the truck? I sure as shit don't have it. And if I did, why would I be riding around with the wallet and screwdriver?"

L.T. was satisfied that Elvis was not a bad liar. A bad liar would fumble over details when pressed to be specific, be unable to match them to the original story. But Elvis Wood had answers for all questions, and detailed answers. That did not prove that he was not lying. But L.T. knew that this man was either an extremely good liar, or he was telling the truth. The latter disturbed him most.

As the evening drew on, Carla and the cowboy talked and danced and laughed and drank. She was still a little hot over the way he made her crawl to him, but as they grew more and more familiar she knew she had to have this man tonight. Wade Burton hauled freight for a terminal in his hometown of McAlester, Oklahoma. He claimed to be one-quarter Cherokee Indian, which probably accounted for the chiseled facial features that attracted women.

"Are you a real cowboy, Wade, or are you just wearing that hat to impress me?"

"Of course, I'm a cowboy. But if I really wanted to impress you, I'd show you my rope."

"I'm not so sure I want to see it. I mean, sure, a rope is long but it's so damn skinny."

"Don't worry, Angel. Mine has a big knot on the end. I guarantee you'll know it's in there."

They laughed aloud. Carla grabbed his hand and dragged him out onto the dance floor. "Oh," she cooed, 'it's Nat Pearce, my all time favorite. Don't you just love her?"

"But she's so old. She's way past her prime, definitely on the downhill side of her career. Stick with the young ones like the Dixie Chicks, Shania Twain. They'll be around a whole lot longer."

Now he was losing points. And the more he drank, the more he put his foot in his mouth. "So tell me, Angel. What brings you to the Buckeye State?"

"Same as you."

"I seriously doubt that."

"It's true, I'm an LTD."

"A what?"

"A lady truck driver."

"Well, then we are the same. I'm an LTD too. A long-tongue driver." He extended it and wiggled it up and down in a practiced, licking motion. As they danced he rubbed and squeezed her tight buttocks through the thin dress. She ground her crotch against his leg until he could feel its warmth, until she could feel his hardness poking and prodding her stomach. When the dance ended they walked with an arm around each other, swaying with the booze, the music, and the raging hormones.

"How the hell does a chick end up driving an eighteen-wheeler? It's about as much a woman's job as a cattle drive."

"Fuck you." She pushed him into his chair and he was losing more points.

"I mean it. The next thing you know, we'll be giving them PMS pay, maternity leave, tampon allowance. Christ."

Carla fumed, but kept her cool. She was not about to give up a chance to ride this stud. Hell, there was no one else worth boinking in the joint. But she knew she would have to teach him a lesson, too. "Let's get out of here."

"Sure, Angel. Say, you're not really a truck driver, are you?" He was a little wobblier as she helped him outside. They flagged a taxi and rode back to her motel.

As they crossed the parking lot, Carla asked, "Wade, have you ever done it in a reefer?"

"In a reefer? Shit, no. The floor's too hard. Trust a woman to come up with a new use for a trailer."

"I want to do it. Come on." She grabbed his hand and led him to the rear of her trailer. She lifted one door latch-handle and swung it open. "Go on in and get ready. I'll go and get us a pillow and blanket." Reluctantly he agreed, having come this far and being so close to getting her out of that tight little dress. He swayed a bit on the way up, but made it in and began to strip. When Carla returned he stood naked in the doorway of the trailer stroking himself. Carla laughed at the long skinny member with its oversize head. It really did look like a rope with a knot in the end. She placed the pillow and blanket in the trailer at his feet then stood on the ground and hiked her dress up in front to make him aware that she had shucked her panties. He whistled and continued to stroke with one hand, reached the other down to help her up and in. As she came up she couldn't resist grabbing his cock with her free hand and pretending to pull herself up with it.

Carla carried the blanket to the nose of the trailer. She slipped her dress over her head and felt the September evening chill caress her bare buttocks and breasts. Wade approached, his right hand still pistoning slowly. Carla sat on the blanket and slid the pillow under her ass. She leaned back and said, "Come and get it, cowboy."

"I don't know," Wade shook his head. "Word gets out I fucked a truck driver, I could be ruined in these parts."

"You don't get over here and give me a rope burn, you're going to lose some of your favorite parts. Come on," she whispered, "bring me that long tongue, driver."

He managed to get his knees onto the edge of the blanket and buried his face in her bush.

Ruby was late closing up the diner. The time she lost at the White Falls Savings and Loan dealing with Ned Dunphy was time she usually reserved for daily cleaning. By the time she returned to the diner it was time for lunch rush and she never did get caught up. She was about ready to lock up and leave when she heard a tapping on the glass of the front door. She plodded over and saw two men in suits, one of which was tapping his car keys incessantly on the window.

"Sorry, fellas. We're closed." She pointed at the CLOSED sign on the door.

The one with the keys kept tapping. The other one said, "We know. We just need to talk with you a moment."

"Who are you?"

"We're security for PHD Holdings." He grabbed the hand of the man with the keys to stop his tapping. "Could you let us in, please?" He held up a business card with PHD Holdings on it.

Ruby opened the door. "What is it?"

"Ms. Treatt, have you seen L.T. Stafford? We've been looking for him. He doesn't seem to be in the neighborhood. Would you happen to know where we might find him?"

"What do you want him for?"

"It's a security matter, ma'am. It really doesn't concern you. Where is he?"

"I have no idea," she lied.

"It's important you tell us the truth. You wouldn't be lying to us, would you ma'am?"

"He left early this morning. Didn't say where he was going. I haven't seen him since."

He handed her his business card. "It's extremely important that we talk with him ma'am. Call us immediately if you see him or hear from him. Can we trust you to do that?"

"Of course. I have no reason to lie to you."

"That's good, ma'am. Because we wouldn't want to see anything come between you and your business partners. It could be bad for business. Know what I mean?"

Ruby just stared as the two men left.

L.T enjoyed a quiet dinner with Ray discussing the case and comparing ideas. She refused to show him a copy of the autopsy report until they had finished eating. She knew the morbid details wouldn't upset her but didn't want to risk spoiling L.T.'s first meal in Dade City. There wasn't much in the Medical Examiner's report that surprised him. Death due to a puncture wound which penetrated the left lung and heart causing catastrophic blood loss and cardiac arrest. The only unusual item appeared to be the presence of paraffin on both the clothes and the skin of the deceased. The report went on to say that the paraffin was a common type that is lightly refined and low-grade, similar to candle wax but not quite as free of impurities. Ray dropped him off at the Riverside Motel and told him where to rent a car the next morning. He spent the rest of the evening studying his notes and writing questions as they came to him.

Wade was snoring almost immediately after he climaxed, which was a damn sight too soon for Carla. She had expected a serious ride from the strange-looking rope. Instead, he had pulled it from her mouth, slipped it up her tunnel, made a few short strokes and spewed. She had tried for several minutes to revive his softening rod but he was too far-gone and of no more use to her. She rose and struggled into her dress, jerked the blanket and pillow out from under the drunken cowboy and tossed them out the door onto the asphalt.

"You dumb fuck," she called to him. "You never should have cut me down. I'm the last woman you'll do that to."

Carla climbed down, closed and latched the door, then walked to the tractor. She wobbled in her heels as she hauled herself up onto the catwalk and moved carefully to the front of the trailer. She held the switch for the glow plug a minute, and then fired up the refrigeration unit. Before leaving, she cranked the thermostat to zero degrees Fahrenheit. A few minutes later she happily masturbated to orgasm in the shower.

Chapter Twelve

Carla sat straight up in bed when her travel alarm sounded at four a.m. She listened for a moment until her ears picked up the steady drone of the diesel refrigeration unit. The four-cylinder engine no longer labored under the heavy task of reducing the trailer temperature to zero degrees. The empty trailer cooled quickly with no cargo holding massive amounts of heat energy. She knew that the only thing in that trailer was now as brittle as an icicle. She smiled to herself and slipped on her jeans and flannel shirt, tossed her things in her travel bag and checked out. She was on the road in minutes but decided to stay away from all Interstate Highways as she headed the truck toward Toledo to pick up her load south. She faced a new challenge this particular morning, namely, finding a suitable spot to dispose of the frozen corpse in her trailer. Easing her rig along US20 west, she searched the small towns and villages for just the right configuration. She had no idea what that might be but drove on confidently knowing she would find something. The big rig motored on, through the deserted streets of Elyria, Norwalk, Bellevue and Clyde.

Just past White Falls Carla slowed when she spotted a sign marked 'TRUCKS TURNING'. She wheeled a wide left into the broad driveway past a sign that marked the entrance to Hennessey Sand and Gravel. She rolled the truck slowly by the unlit trailer office and down the grade toward the pit. Then she circled it in front of a mountain of sand to line up the trailer and began backing it toward the pile. She stopped when the trailer's bumper touched the sand pile, tugged on her work gloves, doused all the lights and climbed down. She walked briskly to the rear of the trailer, struggled to climb far enough up the pile to enable her access to the door and swung it open. The reefer was still running, blasting Carla with a sudden shocking wave of icy air. The inside of the trailer immediately fogged up as the warm ambient air drifted in through the open door and mingled with the freezer's contents. She made her way through the frozen mist, slipping and sliding on the icy aluminum floor.

When her foot bumped Wade's frozen carcass her shoes lost their grip on the smooth ribs of the floor and she came down hard on the rigid body. She felt around for something to haul herself back up with. Her hand came upon his frozen penis and she said, "Nice going, Wade. A little late, but nice."

She felt around and gathered up his clothes into a pile on his chest. On her knees behind him in the nose of the trailer she pushed hard against the man. His corpse slid easily across the trailer floor and she encountered no more trouble in getting him off the truck and into the sand pile. She jumped from the trailer to the sand above Wade and used her feet to push enough sand down to cover him. In minutes she had closed the trailer and was rolling west again toward Toledo.

"You dumb fuck." She shook her head and laughed aloud.

Dickie Thompson should have skipped breakfast Thursday morning. He was running late again and knew old man Hennessey would be on his ass if he didn't have his front-end loader fired up and moving sand at six-thirty sharp. But he just couldn't work a shift without a hearty breakfast. The tires screeched on his old Bronco as it skidded to a stop in front of Ruby's Diner. He bounced in and took a stool at the counter, waving at Harmon Cooter and his brother Wilfred who sat sipping coffee in a booth.

"Slow down, Dickie. Wouldn't want old Orville to know you could make it to the office on time."

Dickie grinned and called out to Priscilla, "Missy Prissy, I'm ready for the usual." She scribbled on her bill pad and passed his request through the order window, then poured a cup of coffee and set it in front of him.

Wilfred Cooter called out, "You're not quite big enough for her usual, Dickie." A roar of laughter spread through the diner. Dickie looked down at his coffee and hunched his shoulders. In a few minutes Priscilla set a platter before him that held three eggs, biscuits, a half-dozen link sausages and two hotcakes. To the amazement of everyone, the hundred and thirty-five pound man inhaled the entire lot in minutes. He tossed a bill on the counter and was out the door as quickly as he had come in, without so much as a sideways glance at the chuckling Cooter brothers.

When he raced into the pit he was ten minutes late. Two dump trucks were already lined up near the sand pile waiting to be loaded. From the corner of his eye he caught the image of Orville Hennessey watching him from the window of the trailer office. Dickie hopped up into the cab of the loader and fired the Caterpillar engine to drown out any yelling from the old man in case he decided to wander down and embarrass him in front of the drivers. Dickie's right hand worked the lever to raise the bucket as his left spun the steering wheel. The loader shot backward, stopped, then lurched forward with bucket lowered and rammed it into the sand pile. The bucket swiveled upward and as it did its operator caught sight of something bluish in color protruding from the sand. Dickie got down slowly and inched toward the bucket. To his utter astonishment it appeared to look oddly like a man's sex organ. He leaned over it, reached out to brush some of the sand away to uncover the rest of the blue genitalia and part of a man's legs. Dickie jumped backward and stood, mouth agape, staring at the human form in the sand. He looked at his hand that had just touched this thing, horrified at how cold it felt. He screamed and turned, climbed quickly back into the cab, closed the door and pulled the lever to gently tip the bucket forward. Sand began to pour out onto the gravel roadway. Suddenly, as the bucket rotated farther, the naked body of a man fell out and lay face up in front of the loader. Dickie stared at it a moment, belched, then spewed bits of sausage, egg, and the rest of his breakfast all over the inside of the windshield and the cab of his Caterpillar office.

After breakfast L.T. drove his rented car north to the junction of SR50 and Route 98 at the US98 Bridge where the body of Arnold Perkins had been found. He parked on the shoulder beyond the span and walked its length, taking in the view of the road, the river, and the tall weeds that lined its banks. The flow of water under the bridge ran at a slow and gentle pace. Its surface appeared black and shiny as truck stop coffee. No matter how long he gazed into it, his vision could not penetrate the murky waters. He made his way off the bridge and over the guardrail along its approach. He climbed down the embankment from the built-up roadway and through the weeds to an area that had been trampled down some fifty yards from the bridge. L.T. concluded that was where Arnold's remains had been found. The weeds were flattened in a circular pattern with a diameter of maybe thirty feet, no doubt from investigators combing the scene. He moved around the interior of its circumference scanning the ground with his eyes. No sign of a physical conflict was evident, nor could he find so much as a drop of blood. He concluded that although this may have been the spot where Arnold was found, it was most certainly not the location of his death. The body was disposed of here.

Elvis Wood said he pulled the dead man from the water. Did the body float here from some entry point up river? he asked himself. No, the autopsy report stated that there was no puffing up of the skin and no bloating, as is the case when a corpse lies in water for a time. That supported Elvis' story about the body entering the river from the bridge then being pulled from the water almost immediately. He scratched out a few more notes and climbed back up to the rental car.

A tall man in a tan-colored uniform stood between the rear of L.T.'s rented Impala and a white police car with green lettering and the insignia of the Pasco County Sheriff's Department.

"You must be Mr. Stafford," the man said from behind dark glasses.

L.T. walked up to him, extended a hand and said, "Good morning. L.T. Stafford."

The officer did not return the gesture of friendship. "Just what do you think you're doing here, Mr. Stafford?"

"Ahh, so you would be Sheriff Henry." He placed his hands on his hips and his smile disappeared. "I was just passing by and needed to go to the bathroom. I didn't see any around so I just went under the bridge to take care of business."

The Sheriff was grinning but L.T. could tell he was not amused. "I got a call from your Chief this morning, Stafford. That is, your former Chief. He tells me they kicked your ass off the police force. He asked me to keep an eye on you, make sure you could find your way home all right. He must really like you. Or something."

L.T.'s eyes narrowed. He couldn't understand why Chief Mackenzie would be looking for him. "I'll be just fine, Sheriff."

"I understand you visited my prisoner yesterday against my orders."

"I'm working for his defense counsel. I was well within the law when I interviewed the suspect."

"Working for Ray White. Well, well. Just what is it you do for her, Stafford? Tote her briefs?" His teeth still showed in a broad grin.

"I'm following up on the accused's account of what happened. Checking its plausibility. Something your department seems to have overlooked."

"We ain't overlooked shit. We just happen to have recovered so much evidence against your boss' client that there's no point in digging any farther. Know what I mean?"

"Aren't you interested in knowing whether his story is true or not?"

"Interested? No. Curious? Maybe. But it just doesn't matter."

"That's a hell of an attitude for a law man."

"Look who's talking to me about attitude. The man who will never work again because he couldn't stand authority. Listen, Stafford, I'm sure you think all I do is sit around and pick my teeth and get fat off the County. Fact is, I'd love to think I've never arrested the wrong man. But this is Pasco County. Folks see a crime like this they want closure. That means justice, hard and fast, whether it's right or wrong because it's right in their eyes. And they're the ones who say whether or not I have a job. Whether he's guilty or innocent Mr. Elvis Wood is going to death row because the people of Pasco County want it that way. That is my job. Truth is not. This is not Ohio. There is no way a jury here would ever acquit his black ass. Now I suggest you conclude your investigation immediately, find a map, and look up the State of Ohio."

L.T. turned and walked around his car and got in without another word. He made a U-turn and headed back toward Dade City with Sheriff Branford Henry following at a distance. For the first time he could remember, the sight of a police car in the rearview mirror made him uneasy. He kept glancing at the reflection wondering what the Sheriff's next move would be. When they passed through Dade, L.T. was relieved to see Henry turn into the parking lot of the

County building. L.T. proceeded south on Route 98 until he picked up Route 301 and followed it south to Zephyrhills, all the while still wondering how Chief Mackenzie knew he was there. And why.

The directions Elvis had given him proved to be right on and L.T. found the ranch without difficulty although he noted that it would be next to impossible to locate if you didn't know exactly where to look. The laneway into the grove was hardly noticeable at all. He eased slowly into the thick tangle of live oaks and Spanish moss. When he spotted the light at the end of this natural tunnel he stopped his car and got out, proceeding on foot to try to avoid being noticed.

He peered out from the grove at the ranch. The unpainted gray clapboard house looked little more than a shack, it's tin roof covered in rust and baked bird droppings. The barn beyond was a larger version of the house. Everything appeared to be shut up tightly but an old, powder blue Chevy van sat near the back porch of the house. He studied the scene for a moment, noting that the barn was easily large enough to hold a tractor-trailer rig. Though the soft, white sand was too delicate to maintain footprints and most tire tracks, wide ruts were visible and indicated the likely presence of large, heavy vehicles such as trucks. He crept on, stepped suddenly into a hole and fell forward cursing aloud, bruising a shin and skinning an elbow on rough wooden planks criss-crossed and standing on edge that had been embedded in the driveway. At first he was certain it was a booby trap but soon realized he had found the cattle gap Elvis had mentioned. So far, Elvis' information was perfectly clear and precise. Maybe too precise, he thought.

L.T. picked himself up, walked carefully across the remaining boards and made his way to the house. He peered through a dirty side window into the kitchen. A round wooden table sat before an L-shaped counter top that hugged two walls. The tabletop bore the marks of years of carving initials and scratching pictures. Three matching chairs sat around it, one pushed completely under the table, the other two left out where they could be used without moving them. He made out a rust-stained porcelain sink and a tin coffee pot sitting on an ancient gas stove. The only sign of recent occupancy was a telephone and answering machine on the counter. He tested the door but it held fast.

His tour continued with a visit to the barn. A large padlock secured the sliding vehicle door so he made his away along the side, found an unlocked window and swung it open. The barn's dark interior brightened slightly by the yellow beams of light that filtered in through the cracks between the boards. He hoisted himself up and in the window, slipped on a galvanized bucket as he lowered himself inside and fell flat, the bucket clattering loudly beside him. He stood up and looked around, giving his eyes a moment to adjust to the darkness. Both sidewalls of the barn were lined with stalls and mangers for livestock. Cattle, he figured, as the stalls were very small and close together, though they showed no sign of having been occupied in recent past. The wide center area of the building remained clear of obstruction with a large sliding door at either end, a drive-thru truck maintenance bay, he surmised.

Only one unusual item caught his eye and stood out from the monotone. A bright red mechanic's tool chest on a matching roller cabinet stood along one side of the drive-thru. He walked over and pulled open a drawer studying the array of hand tools. The chest and the cabinet of tools were all the same brand: Crafters. L.T. squinted to make notes in the darkness. Nothing else seemed notable so he climbed back out the window and headed back to his car. He took a last look around and could find nothing really out of the ordinary about the place except that it was kind of spooky being so well hidden. The rusted hulks of three stripped-down old truck tractors lay deteriorating under the sun in the pasture behind the barn. The place just appeared to be an old ranch that some independent trucker now called home and tried to make a living from.

Back at the Riverside Motel he dialed Florida Highway Patrol. He managed to reach Trooper Warden Trout with whom he had spoken earlier about the disappearance of Ruby's brother. He had very thoughtfully called L.T. back when word first arrived of the body being found.

"Hey, Sergeant Stafford. How's the weather in Ohio?"

"Can't say, Trout. I'm right here in beautiful downtown Dade City."

"Welcome to Florida, Officer. I take it then you have met Sheriff Henry."

"Oh, yes, the Sheriff has made his presence known to me. In fact, he was kind enough to offer me a map of Ohio."

Trout laughed. "That's the head of Pasco County's finest for you. What can I help you with, officer?"

"Any new information you could offer to help me get to the bottom of this homicide? I realize this is not a Highway Patrol matter, that it's Henry's investigation but I thought I'd take a chance on you anyway."

"As a matter of fact, there may be something. A mechanic at the truck stop up in Wildwood was out behind the shop having a smoke yesterday and managed to wrest a bloodstained sneaker away from a dog. One of our officers happened to be gassing up at the time so the man handed it over to him. We, of course, sent a sample to Tampa for DNA testing. In checking with Pasco County we discovered that the shoe was the same brand and size as the one Perkins was wearing. He had a left, we found a right. Wildwood is up in Sumter County beyond Sheriff Henry's jurisdiction so he was not directly involved. However, we felt we had enough reason to conduct a search of the area. Upon doing so, we discovered a relatively large area of what appeared to be blood stains on the asphalt at the very rear of the truck parking area. Onsite testing later revealed it was, in fact, human blood. Someone lost a life there. Fortunately, we've had no rain in several days. Samples again were taken. DNA profiling from these samples will be compared against each other and also with those collected from any unidentified corpses and unsolved homicides throughout the state. They also will be provided to the FBI's National Center for the Analysis of Violent Crime for use in the VICAP system. You're familiar with VICAP, Sergeant Stafford?"

"Violent Criminal Apprehension Program, yes. When do you expect the results of testing?"

"That's never certain. The lab in Tampa is awfully busy. Could be anywhere from a few days to three weeks. I have your number. I'll be certain to call as soon as we get a report."

"So, it sounds like he was killed at the truck stop in Wildwood and dumped at the US98 Bridge."

"That's the theorization to date. It also fits with what we got from the shipper at Brooksville where the victim was due to pick up a load Saturday morning. The man said the driver had called Friday afternoon to say that he would be spending the night at the truck stop and would be at Brooksville first thing in the morning. Of course, he never made it. You're probably aware the Medical Examiner couldn't pinpoint time of death but calculated it to be sometime Friday evening. Almost everything we found pointed to the Perkins homicide, including one other crucial piece of evidence."

"What do you mean?"

"We recovered a thirty-eight caliber slug from the pavement near the blood-stained area. At first we thought the victim had been shot but the M.E. reported the puncture wound was a stabbing. That also fit with the murder weapon Sheriff Henry found in the suspect's possession. Analysis revealed, though, that the gun that fired the bullet was pointed at a downward angle of a hundred and forty degrees. Our investigators suggest it was likely pointed that way as a result of a struggle and went off during the fracas. We later learned that the M.E. found gunpowder residue on the victim's right hand indicating he had fired a gun."

"So he didn't go down easy."

"There's just one thing that seems queer. If the gun was fired at a downward angle of a hundred and forty degrees it means the attacker would have come at him from the front and forced his arm down and to the side. But the entrance wound from the screwdriver was in the victim's back. How do you figure that?"

"Either the assailant subdued him, got him down and stabbed him from behind or..."

"Or?" asked Trout.

"Or he had an accomplice." L.T. thanked him and hung up. He leaned back on the bed and flipped through his notebook, absentmindedly mulling over the thought of how good a cold beer would taste. It suddenly struck him that he had been so caught up in everything that he hadn't had a drink in days. Not since Sunday night, the eve of the day his life changed forever had he tasted alcohol. Funny, this time he had hardly noticed the dry mouth, the quivering hands, and the cold sweats. He stepped outside into the searing mid-day sun and retrieved a Coke from the vending machine, then returned to his notes.

How does a man on a motorcycle transport a two-hundred-pound dead man some thirty-five miles? With a stolen truck? Where's the truck? If he sold the truck, where's the money? Why does a small-town fisherman kill a trucker? And if he does, why does he have to transport him thirty-five miles before disposing of him? The questions kept bouncing around in his mind but any possible answers he plugged in kept discounting the notion that Elvis Wood killed Arnold Perkins. He took his Coke and headed for the truck stop at Wildwood.

It took a little more than an hour to reach the truck stop. L.T. was mesmerized by the size and by the number of trucks that just kept coming in and going out as he watched. It was past one p.m. and the smell of country-fried steak and biscuits drew him out of the parking lot and into the restaurant for lunch. He showed the waitress the picture of Arnold that Ruby had given him and asked her to show it around. No one recalled seeing the man. After eating he talked with the attendant at the fuel desk and the mechanic who found the shoe. Not one person recognized the man in the picture. L.T. studied the photo. Sure, it's a big place with hundreds of truck drivers in and out every day, he thought, but somebody would have remembered a mug as homely as this. He shook his head and returned to his car.

Before leaving, he decided to take a look around the parking lot. He drove slowly up and down the rows of tractor-trailer rigs of all descriptions, concluding that there were a great many blue Kenworths that looked like Gary Turner's. He swung around into the last row between trucks and spotted a familiar rig. It was the silver Freightliner and flatbed trailer of Diesel Doobie. The windows were up but the engine was idling. He got out and knocked on the driver's door. In a moment, Doobie appeared from the sleeper, naked from at least the waist up which was all L.T. could see from where he stood on the ground.

The driver opened a window and called out, "Hey, co-driver. Are you ready to head back up north to the Buckeye State?"

L.T. thought about it. "When are you leaving?"

"Probably about this time tomorrow. Have to load down at Naples first thing in the morning. Picking up four hundred bags of cypress mulch for a landscaper in Toronto. Can you believe that? Cypress from the everglades on the lawns of the doctors and lawyers of Toronto. Times have changed. Used to be manure. Now it's cypress mulch. Still horseshit if you ask me but it pays. How about it? You driving?"

"Let me think about it. I have your number."

A woman's head poked out from the sleeper, followed by her naked breasts. She slid onto Doobie's lap and smiled out at L.T.

"Hey, Suzie, this is my co-driver L.T. L.T. you want to take Suzie for a spin?"

He laughed and turned and got back in his car, shaking his head. On the drive back to Dade City more questions began bouncing around and searching for answers in the farthest regions of his mind. It looked to him like maybe Arnold was accosted before he even had a chance to enter the truck stop building. He was killed in the very back row of the parking lot, which meant he was probably parked there. Since he never made it inside, he wasn't there long. The whole thing was beginning to smell of a setup. But by whom, and for what reason? Who would plan an ambush of a driver of an empty truck?

Who was this couple at the ranch? How did they fit in? Did they really dump the body or were they just a couple that Elvis fingered to save himself from execution. It looked increasingly like he was not guilty of murder but may still be a cunning liar in his own defense. And the ranch had turned into a dead end, so to speak.

Chapter Thirteen

From his room he called Claude Primeau at New York Truck Brokers.

"Hi, officer. Find that missing truck yet? We heard about the farmer. Tough luck. Guess he wasn't gypsying after all."

"How long has Turner worked for you?"

"Not long, best part of a year, give or take. I could look it up for you."

"Not necessary. How well do you know him?"

"Well, you've got to appreciate I only see these guys for a couple minutes every two weeks or so. And there's so much damn turnover in this business. New hires, guys quitting because the grass is greener at East Coast Freight. But they got shittier runs, I'll guarantee you. I guess, you really don't get to know your drivers any more, not like you used to. They come and they go."

"Was he a good worker?"

"Still is. I got him doing fill in. You know, vacation runs like the farmer did."

"Was he ever in trouble?"

"Nothing showed up on his background check. We look at criminal records before we hire. You just never know these days."

"What about money? Is he financially solvent?"

"Solvent? Solvent we use to remove grease from engines, transmissions, rear axles. What the hell is solvent?"

"Did he have enough money?"

"Shit, does anybody? Come to think of it, we had a lot of trouble with this guy when he first came on. An ex-wife in Pennsylvania is still garnishing him for payment of alimony and child support. This guy was always asking for advances. How he managed credit for a new Kenworth tractor and stainless steel Great Dane is beyond me. Oh, wait; it was some kind of insurance payment. Yeah, come to think of it, I think his last truck was stolen."

"Did he carry theft insurance on the new truck?"

"Of course, that's a requirement."

L.T. got the address of Gary Turner from Primeau before hanging up and asked him not to mention their conversation to the driver. He arranged to meet Ray for dinner to discuss the details of his investigation to date. Leaning back on the bed, he surfed the television channels, settling on an afternoon newscast from Tampa. Although he had slept better the previous night than he had in recent memory, cumulative insomnia was overtaking him and he dozed repeatedly. The words 'White Falls, Ohio' jarred him awake, and he sat up blinking at the set. There on the screen was the image of little Dickie Thompson standing next to his loader in Hennessey's gravel pit. The giant machine made him look even smaller, as did the tall, red-haired woman who interviewed him. L.T. fumbled with the volume control.

"Police are baffled by the discovery of a frozen human corpse found within this giant mound of sand near White Falls. Dickie Thompson, operator of this loading machine uncovered the body. Mr. Thompson, what was your initial reaction upon making this grisly find?"

Overload

"I puked. Blew my breakfast all over the inside of the cab. I never seen anything like this before. Uh, then I called the cops."

"State and local police are working together in an effort to identify the victim." The newscaster took a few steps and the camera followed to reveal Chief Conrad Mackenzie. "With me now is Chief Mackenzie of the White Falls Police Department. Chief can you tell us if foul play is suspected?"

"Well now, it would be pretty difficult to rule out foul play in this case. A man doesn't climb into a sand pile naked and freeze himself in seventy-eight degree weather. This is definitely a homicide."

"Thank you Chief Mackenzie. The unidentified victim is male, Caucasian, in his thirties. Police for now are calling him the iceman. This is Virginia Barker reporting live from Ohio."

L.T. sat stunned, his jaw gaping, still staring at the television. "How the hell does a man freeze to death in September in White Falls?" Thoughts of how a person might freeze danced about in his brain. Was he alive when someone froze him? Was he killed and then stored in a freezer? Were there signs of trauma on the body? Has he been reported missing? Who the hell was he? It was definitely time to return home, being drawn there by the prospect of quizzing Gary Turner about his truck insurance, by Ruby's money laundering problems, by the apparent suicide of his friend Kendall Griffith, and now by the iceman.

As L.T. fumbled through his suitcase in search of something presentable to wear to dinner with Raylene White he noticed a car pull up to the office, an airport rental car judging by the Hertz signage on the back.

Two men in suits got out and looked around. They were familiar somehow. Then he remembered and moved to the window to draw the drapes. Peering out from behind them, he saw the same two men Connie Mackenzie had been talking to at Kendall Griffith's the morning he was found hanged. The men entered the motel office and came out a moment later with the desk clerk who pointed in the direction of L.T.'s room. As they moved slowly toward him, one pulled a gun. L.T. scanned the room quickly for a weapon, found none. He ran into the bathroom, ripped the ceramic towel bar off the drywall and went back to the door and stood behind it. A heavy knock sounded. Then another.

"Mr. Stafford, it's hotel security. We need to have a word with you."

L.T. wrinkled his brow and mouthed the words silently, "Hotel security my ass."

The door burst open. L.T. waited for the first man to take a step in then slammed the door back against him with all his weight behind it. It caught him square in the nose and forehead staggering him. L.T. pulled back on the door and let him have it again. The gun fell to the floor and L.T. snatched it up. He swung the door one more time, dragged the staggering man in the suit through it and whacked him once on the back of the head with the ceramic towel bar. The stranger dropped like a felled tree. L.T. quickly knelt and put the gun barrel to his head.

"Drop it now or your pal's dead meat," he called out to the other man who was about to enter the door with gun blazing. Caught off guard he stopped short.

After a second of consideration, the man dropped his weapon.

"Now get your ass in here."

The second suit stepped over his unconscious colleague and stood beside him near the bed.

"Who are you guys and what do you want?"

"Donald Duck, Mickey Mouse, and your ass."

L.T. stood up, gun in one hand, ceramic towel bar in the other. "Turn around and face the wall," he shouted. The stranger didn't move, just stood smirking at him. "Fuck it, then, don't turn around." With a wrist shot rivaling Brett Hull he whacked the man across the left temple with the motel towel bar once, twice, and before the third swing the smartass hit the floor face down across his fallen partner. L.T. bent down and pulled both wallets from their pockets, fished out the driver licenses and slipped them in his trouser pocket. He dropped the wallets and picked up both guns, the towel bar and his suitcase and tossed them in his car. Just for good measure he pulled the keys out of their rental car, checked out of the Riverside Motel and called Ray White on his cell phone to beg off dinner and convince her to go to Wildwood with him. He made one final call to Diesel Doobie, who promised not to leave town without him.

L.T. drove straight to Ray White's office to pick her up.

"You're early," she said. "Just give me a minute." She disappeared into an inner office. When she emerged a few minutes later she had traded her blue business suit for tight jeans and a strapless white bustier. L.T. sucked in a breath at the vision of her golden hair falling on freckled shoulders. He gazed at the pattern of those freckles and how they drew his eyes off her round shoulders to highlight the sumptuous cleavage as it disappeared into her top. She plucked her keys from her purse on the desk then swung around and bent over to pick up her briefcase. As L.T. admired her broad hips and round buttocks he couldn't help wondering if the move was planned. When they went out the door, Ray handed the briefcase to L.T. while she locked up.

L.T. chuckled and she gave him an inquisitive look. "When I told Sheriff Henry I was working for you he asked if I toted your briefs."

"What makes you and the sheriff think I wear any?" She winked at him and headed out the door. "Give me your keys. I'll show you the neighborhood."

He handed them to her and said, "You can drive, but let's just get to Wildwood."

"You seem in an awful hurry to leave."

"I just had a visit from some very unfriendly folks."

Ray pulled out of the parking lot and headed up US98. "What? Sheriff Henry leaning on you?"

He handed her the driver's licenses from the two men in suits. She studied them as she drove. "Alonzo Morgan and Salvatore Gambino. Never heard of them." She checked their addresses. "Atlantic City. A couple of all-American boys. What did they want with you?"

"I'm not sure. But I saw them in White Falls a few days ago. I took these from them today." He showed her the guns.

"Jesus," she said. "You must have really pissed off the mayor when you whooped his ass."

He just stared at her. When they passed the Riverside Motel, Ray slowed to look at a small crowd gathering around an ambulance and two Sheriff's cars.

"Don't slow down," he said. "By now the Sheriff will be looking for me."

"What did you do? Kill those guys?"

"No. I just hit them."

"What with? A truck?"

He reached behind the seat and showed her the towel bar.

"I must remember never to get into the shower with you," she said.

"I would never use that on you, Ray."

"Sure. Some other deadly weapon, I suppose."

He smiled and it felt good. "Think you could check out Morgan and Gambino for me? I don't have access to those services any more."

She slipped the licenses into her purse. "I wish you weren't leaving so soon. I could really use your help."

"You've still got my help. I'm going north in search of a killer."

"Then you believe Elvis' story?"

"No matter how you look at it, he's got no motive. Everything Henry has on him is circumstantial."

"I'm afraid that's plenty for a conviction in Pasco. That means the only way to save Wood is to find the killer. What have you got up yonder?"

"I'm not sure, yet. But it seems like Perkins was set up for ambush before he got to the truck stop. I want to find out if the owner had anything to do with it. We know it wasn't a hijacking. The trailer wasn't loaded.

Maybe it was an insurance job. Maybe the owner needed to get out from under the heavy payments."

"What about this couple at the ranch in Zephyrhills? How do they figure into this?"

"So far that's the only part of his story that doesn't seem to fit. I went there – to the ranch – but there was nothing out of the ordinary. No one around so I couldn't ask any questions and no trucks there either, although there were signs that trucks had been there. But it just looked like some poor slob trucker was trying to make a living from there. See if you can find out whose place it is, get some background."

Ray nodded. "Shouldn't be too difficult. Maybe that poor slob trucker is making a living with a stolen truck. I'll put a little pressure on the District Attorney. I'm sure she'll at least make the Sheriff check their truck to see if it's stolen. Any idea about the paraffin on the victim's body? It was mentioned in the autopsy report."

"Haven't a clue."

They approached the US98 Bridge and L.T. asked her to stop halfway across. He tossed the guns and the towel bar over the rail, and then motioned for Ray to drive on. When they reached Wildwood he rented a room at the Days Inn. This time he paid with cash so he couldn't be traced. Then they walked across SR44 to the truck stop to have dinner at Ray's suggestion.

L.T. looked surprised. "I just don't see you as someone who would eat in a truck stop."

"Hell," she replied, "I've represented truckers. I even know one or two cuss words."

They laughed and chatted for a couple hours. L.T. was feeling comfortable with Ray and wished he didn't have to leave. After dinner she walked him back to the motel. He thanked her for returning his rental car and she made him promise to come back and take her for a real dinner. Then she kissed him softly on the lips and left.

From his room he called Doobie, who promised to pick him up at the truck stop on the way back from Naples Friday afternoon. He settled in to study his notes and after a few minutes was startled by a knock at the door. He opened it to find Ray standing there.

"So what?" she asked. "You don't find me attractive?" She entered the room, closed the door behind her and wrapped her arms around his neck as she kissed him. She kicked off her shoes and started moving forward, still kissing him deeply, pushing him toward the bed. Her hands went to her waist and fumbled with the button on her jeans. With L.T.'s help she tugged them over her hips and stepped out of them. She lifted the bustier over her head as L.T. struggled out of his clothes. Her mouth locked on his again. Ray pushed him back on the bed and climbed atop him. Her fingers wrapped around his rigid penis, stroked it a couple of times, then guided it into her steamy wetness. Her hips ground against him and he rose to meet each thrust. Sweat trickled down off her breasts to mingle with his. They rode wildly, each sensing the other's impending climax and grinding harder and deeper. When they finally came she collapsed atop him then slid to the side and lay with her head on his muscular shoulder, her fingers entwined in his graying chest hairs.

They lay together for an hour, quietly caressing arms, legs, necks, buttocks. Then L.T. turned to gently kiss her and their temperatures began to rise again. He was grateful that she had given him time to recover from their first adventure. They continued to kiss and she reached for his penis to massage and stroke it to life again. It didn't take long and L.T. mounted her. Softly and slowly they made love.

Chapter Fourteen

Carla was offloaded and home by suppertime Friday. The rig rolled gently to a stop in the barn, the hissing sounds of air brakes reverberating off wooden walls. The Caterpillar diesel shuddered and quaked, then quieted as she shut it down. She sat there in the shadows of the barn for a moment, hands still on the wheel and said aloud, "God, I love this truck." Without moving from the seat she reached behind with her right hand and plucked her leather travel bag from the sleeper compartment, picked up her paperwork from the clipboard on the doghouse and climbed down.

Marlin rolled in about eleven-thirty. He found Carla in the living room watching a movie in the dark and sucking on her third beer.

"Hey," was all he said to her.

"Hey yourself."

He grabbed one from the refrigerator, popped the top and sat at the kitchen table. His sister wandered in, beer in hand, wearing only a tee shirt and took a seat. Marlin opened his leather folder, pulled out a newspaper clipping from Chatsworth, Georgia and slid it across the table toward her."

"What's this?" she asked. "Your obituary notice?"

"Not mine, smartass. Read it."

She scanned the two-paragraph story about the accidental death of a computer salesman whose car had slipped off its jack and pinned him. Georgia Highway Patrol were asking anyone who witnessed the accident or who had any information to contact them.

"So what?" she said.

"So what? So, that's the dude that cut me off. He won't do that again."

"Wow," she said, without emotion again.

"What the fuck is this wow shit, Carla? Oh, I get it. It's a putdown. Fine. You figure you can just keep putting me down. Fine. Take another look at that. 'Accidental death'. Get what that means, Carla? It means the cops don't even come looking for me or anyone else over this. You think you're smart. This is smart."

"This still doesn't even prove you were there. Why should I believe you? Why should anyone? You could have happened along after this accident and gone back later for the newspaper."

"I'm telling you, I fucking did this."

"Look, Fish. You want to impress me, right? That's what this is all about?"

"I'm telling you we're even, Carla. That's all. You killed a guy. I killed a guy. We're even. I'm the boss of this company."

"Yeah, whatever. Only, we'll never be even."

"What?"

"In the first place, I killed to save your life. You, on the other hand, killed only because I killed. That's hardly noble, or even important. Furthermore, I've killed twice, not once like you."

"Bullshit."

"Bullshit?" She reached for her purse on the counter and retrieved Wade Burton's Teamsters card and handed it to him.

"What's this?"

"Read about it in the Tribune tomorrow. Not some hick-town rag, the Tampa Tribune." She picked up her beer and headed for the living room.

L.T. reached White Falls Saturday morning at about eleven and headed straight for the diner. The two men had again shared the driving, with L.T. playing a more prominent role as his confidence and comfort behind the wheel surged with each shift. Doobie was grateful and repaid the kindness by going out of his way to deliver L.T. to his hometown. The Explorer still awaited repairs in Lexington. Doobie parked the rig across from the diner and the two men walked in together.

"Yeah, this is the place," said Doobie. "But that ain't Ruby."

L.T. stared at the chunky blonde woman with enormous breasts threatening to burst from her uniform. The place was empty and she sat chewing gum and reading the paper behind the counter.

"What can I get you boys?" she asked without genuine interest.

"Excuse me," said L.T. "Where's – could I talk to – is Ruby here?"

"'Fraid not. She's at a funeral in New York. She'll be back Monday morning. Anything I can do for you?" She raised an eyebrow.

"What about Priscilla?"

"She ain't here either. She quit."

"Quit? Priscilla?"

"Just the other day. So I'm here to take her place, Acting Manager while Ruby's away. You boys want anything? Some coffee maybe?"

"No, I think I'll just head on upstairs. I'm L.T. Stafford. I live in the apartment upstairs."

"Aha," said the waitress, "So you're the one."

"Which one is that, ma'am?"

"The one occupying my new apartment."

"What?"

"Oh, right. You've been out of town and didn't get the notice. Well, I expect you'll get it shortly."

L.T. could feel his lower jaw hanging loose. He looked at Doobie, who just shrugged and said, "Shit happens, eh."

They walked out and stood on the sidewalk a moment. Doobie said, "Listen, I'm heading back down first of the week. If you need work or a place to stay, well I got this motor home."

L.T. shook his hand and did his best to smile. "Thanks for everything, Doobie. Who knows? Things don't cool down here I may have to take you up on that. Meanwhile, motor safely, my friend." He watched as Doobie climbed into the silver Freightliner then called out to him, "Keep the shiny side up."

Doobie gave a quick blast of the air horn and rolled the big rig away with black smoke blowing. L.T. walked into the alley carrying his suitcase and shaking his head. As he climbed the stairs he noticed a car turning into the alley down the block. A black Chrysler stopped halfway up the alley but no one got out. L.T. continued up the stairs and noticed his front door ajar. He put down his suitcase and slowly opened the screen door. It creaked and he froze. Nothing happened so he pulled it wide and crept in. The place looked like a garbage truck had been through and unloaded in his living room. Pictures, cushions, contents of drawers, books, magazines, dishes, mail, all strewn about the floor. Every room had been trashed.

"Looks like you could use a housekeeper."

He wheeled, ready for a fight but the soft voice was that of a pretty young woman in her mid-thirties. "Sorry. Didn't mean to startle you. I can see why you'd be a bit jumpy though. Or is this the way it always looks?"

L.T.'s jaw dropped again. She was much younger, but bore a striking resemblance to Natalie Pearson, now Nat Pearce the Nashville Nightingale, his high school sweetheart. They had vowed to love each other forever. He blinked and shook his head.

"Who are you?"

"Are you Luke Stafford?"

He nodded, jaw still gaping.

"Then I guess I'm your daughter." She extended a hand. "Hey. I'm Cheryl Pearson."

A loud creak sounded from a board on the stairs outside. L.T. pointed to his bedroom and said, "Quick, in there." He peered out the window and saw the two bruised men in suits from the Riverside Motel. "Well, if it isn't hotel security," he said under his breath. Both men approached slowly with guns drawn. L.T. looked around, stepped quickly into the kitchen and grabbed a bottle of Crisco Oil from the cupboard. He twisted the top off and tossed it on the floor just inside the front door. Its contents puddled on the vinyl flooring. He knelt down and unscrewed a leg from the coffee table and crouched behind the recliner next to the open door. This time the smartass entered first. He stepped in the cooking oil and his feet flew forward. He came down hard on his back, his skull striking the two-by-six doorsill with a crack and he never moved again. His partner with the broken nose was holding the screen door open and stopped to look down at him for just a second too long. L.T. sprang upright and whacked the man's gun hand with the table leg. The weapon fell on the porch with a clatter as the man cried out in pain. Before he could get his hands up to defend himself, L.T. caught him under the chin with the wooden leg. He staggered backward with L.T. following in his face. That powerful right that had cost the mayor a new bridge and L.T. his job drove him and the broken nose did a back flip over the railing, landing in the dumpster at the back of the diner.

L.T. turned to see Cheryl watching wide-eyed and grinning.

"Awesome," she said. "Primitive but totally deadly."

He grabbed her by the arm and pulled her, saying, "Let's get out of here. The new tenant can clean this shithole."

"Where are we going?" she asked, as they ran down the alley.

"Ever been to New York?"

"New York City?"

"More like Rutland Center."

"Never heard of it."

"You'll love it."

When Marlin returned from the grocery store he found Carla in the barn using a stepladder to wash the windows on her truck. She leaned across the hood to scrub the bugs off the windshield and he found himself unable to resist the urge to run a hand up her shorts and squeeze the soft, molded flesh of her left buttock.

"Who is it?" she teased.

He tossed the newspaper onto the hood of the truck. It was opened to the national page and she scanned it for the header. Halfway down the page she read, 'Police in Ohio Baffled by Frozen Corpse'.

"What's this all about, Carla? No bullshit."

She turned on the ladder and looked down at him. "It's one thing to kill a guy and make people believe it's an accident. But it's a work of art when people know it's murder yet have no clue how or why or who done it."

"This guy, Wade Burton. You have his driver's union card. They say he's from Oklahoma. You killed this guy?"

"Dead."

"You did it in this reefer, didn't you?"

"Did."

"Why?"

"Fish, if I have to explain, you wouldn't understand."

"What kind of bullshit is that, Carla?"

"Remember that night at the truck stop when the guy had the gun pointed at you and you just knew you were dead?"

"Yeah, so what?"

"How did you feel?"

"Shit-scared. More shit-scared than when the old man came home drunk."

"How about when that guy that you knew was going to kill you fell dead at your feet from my hands?"

"Better. Alive again. Still scared, but not shit-scared."

"How did you feel when you did the asshole with the BMW?"

He looked up at her and raised his hands. "Like I just won the Daytona 500. Like I just won the LOTTO. Like I fucking killed Bin Laden. Like nothing I ever felt before." His hands were shaking now.

"The world is full of assholes, Fish. There's just three less assholes now. Why don't we stop this crazy fighting and just run our trucks?"

He reached up and put his hands on her knees then slid them upward slowly feeling his fingertips vibrate along the silky expanse of her thighs, tingling like they had electricity flowing through them. His fingers traveled up, up into the legs of her shorts and stopped to linger a moment on the bush. He leaned in and inhaled her fragrance, its heavy scent filling his nostrils, as she wore no panties. Slowly he slid the shorts down her thighs, over her knees, and to her ankles without drawing back his face. She placed her hands in his hair and drew him in.

The sound of a car door slamming surprised them and they scrambled to compose themselves. Marlin walked out of the barn to find two Pasco County Sheriff's deputies standing next to a patrol car.

"Good day, deputies."

"Are you Mr. Sears?" one of them asked.

"That I am," Marlin replied coolly.

"And is this the address of Sears Refrigerated Transport?"

"It is."

"This company owns two tractor-trailer rigs. Is that right sir?"

"Oh yeah. A '97 model Kenworth and '94 Trailmobile reefer, and a 2000 Kenworth with a '99 Great Dane reefer."

"Would that be the 1997 Kenworth over there beside the barn?"

"Yeah, that's the one I drive."

The deputy motioned for his partner to go and take a look at the truck, then said, "You don't mind if we have a look, do you?"

"Aren't you supposed to have a warrant or something?"

"Technically, yes. But that's just a formality. If you refuse we'll just set out there by the road, wait for you to pull out and haul you over. At least if we do it this way, you're not made a spectacle for your neighbors to gossip over."

Marlin shrugged his shoulders. "Guess you might as well get after it then."

"Where is the other rig?"

"Oh, it's in the barn. Through that door, deputy."

Carla had been peering out through a crack in the barn boards and chose that moment to come out of the barn topless. When the deputy caught sight of her swaying breasts he stopped dead in his tracks. Carla feigned surprise and made a half-hearted attempt to cover her bosom with crossed arms but made sure there were nipple-gaps in her coverage. The deputy blushed but couldn't take his eyes off her.

"Howdy, Ma'am. Are you Mrs. Sears?"

"That would be Ms. I'm the sister and the other driver. She held out a hand to shake and uncovered her right breast. "Oops," she said, and crossed her arms again.

"I need to have a look at your truck, Miss." The deputy was blushing now.

"Y'all just go right ahead, Hon. I'll see if I can find that shirt of mine. It's here in the barn somewhere."

He followed her in, enjoying the bounce in her buttocks and the smooth, clean lines of her naked back and shoulders. She retrieved her tee shirt from the left fender but before she got a chance to slip it over her head he said, "I'll need to see your registration, Miss."

"Alrighty, Officer," she sang. She climbed up into the cab, dropping the effort at modesty. Retrieving the pink slip from the leather pocket on the doghouse she swung around in the seat with her breasts jiggling and handed it to him. "Anything else you need to see, Hon?"

He smiled at her chest but couldn't say a word. He compared the Vehicle Identification Number on the registration to the VIN plate on the door and noted that they matched. "You, uh, you have the trailer papers, Miss?"

"Oh, sure, Hon," she drawled and swung to reach for them. Just for emphasis she leaned over so that her buttocks became visible out the legs of her shorts. He gasped, then cleared his throat to cover up. Carla swung back and handed him the trailer registration. He walked over and compared the number with the VIN plate on the Great Dane.

"Everything all right, Sugar?"

"Oh, yeah, I mean yes." He returned to stand below her at the side of the cab and spoke to her breasts. "We, uh, we got a report of a rig like this stolen up the country last week so we're just checking everything in the area that matches the description. "You're fine, though. All your numbers check out just fine."

She chuckled. "Well, who would know better than you, Hon?"

He smiled and turned to walk out of the barn.

L.T. and Cheryl piled into the rented Camry she had picked up at the airport in Cleveland and began slowly to share their stories. They would talk for a bit then stop, neither one knowing just what to say to bridge the awkward silences. L.T. could feel the guilt welling up inside him. He wanted to tell her he had no idea she existed until this very day, and that if he had known he would have been with her mother from the beginning. He wanted to tell her a thousand things just didn't know how.

She still lived with her mother in Goodlettsville, Tennessee just outside Nashville. She worked as a backup singer for her Mom but had cut a CD of her own under the name Cheryl Dakota. She had an ex-husband named Nathan Perry who was a rat. And she had no children. L.T. told her that was a damn good thing since one surprise like this was enough for a while. Grandchildren could come later.

They took turns driving the five hundred miles from White Falls to Rutland Center, driving well into the night. Cheryl asked him what kind of trouble he was in. He told her he wasn't quite certain but that someone was definitely trying to kill him, he knew that now and he figured he might know who but had no idea why. Not yet, anyway. He told her about the fracas with the mayor and losing his job and she said she had heard of the guy and that Natalie just hated him. They stopped for the night at a Motel Six in Erie, Pennsylvania. L.T. hated to ask but had to get Cheryl to pay for the rooms with her credit card, as he was certain someone was monitoring his financial transactions.

He grabbed his suitcase and was about to enter his room when Cheryl said, "Dad?"

He turned toward her, dropped the bag and opened his arms and she fell into them. "You'll never have to come searching for me again, Cheryl. I promise." He gazed into her eyes.

"What? What is it?" she asked.

"God, I can't get over it. You look so much like your mother. Except for your nose, maybe."

"Looks like you're responsible for that." They both chuckled.

"And your voice," he said. "It's as though I were talking to Natalie. You sound just like her."

"You ought to hear me sing."

They embraced for several minutes then retired to their rooms.

After breakfast L.T. and his daughter Cheryl drove the remaining two hours to Rutland Center and paid a visit to Gary Turner. L.T. felt strongly that Turner was behind the disappearance of his truck for the purpose of collecting insurance money and Arnold had been an unwary and unlucky participant. Turner lived in a modest bungalow in the small village of Rutland Center. They found him out front cutting the grass with a push mower. He gave a friendly wave when they pulled in even though he had no idea who the strangers were. He stopped mowing and went over to greet them.

L.T. offered his hand and introduced himself.

"Ah, you're the policeman that called about Arn. I understand you know his sister Ruby."

"That's right. She's a good friend."

"I met her yesterday, at the funeral. Nice lady. But very sad. God, I felt awful about Arn. If I hadn't pestered him to take that run, he'd still be here, working his farm just down the road. He was a great guy. Always bringing us vegetables from his garden, fresh, yard-fed chickens, and eggs. What a guy."

"I'm looking into his death. I'm sure you've heard by now it was homicide."

"Tragic. How can I help, officer?"

"I just need to ask you a few questions. Was your truck insured for theft?"

"Oh, yeah. Nobody will hire you these days if you don't carry full insurance."

"Has your insurance company paid your claim yet?"

"No. I haven't filed a claim yet. I was hoping the rig would be recovered somewhere."

"Have you ever filed a theft claim before?"

"Yes. Two years ago. I was on a run to Seattle and I was hijacked. Beat me up bad. I was in hospital for weeks with a concussion, ruptured spleen, busted ribs and a punctured lung. Sometimes, it's a tough business."

"How is your financial state?"

"What do you mean?"

"Are you having money problems?"

"So that's it. You think I stole my own truck for the insurance money and killed my friend."

"Understand we have to eliminate every possibility."

He looked at the gravel in his driveway. "Did anyone tell you why I didn't want to go on that run?"

L.T. shook his head.

"My wife was desperate to have a child. She's miscarried three times and each time the shock to her system both physically and emotionally did a shitload of damage. This was the first time she carried full term and I had to be with her. She just couldn't go through this without me."

"How did she…" He hesitated. "How is she?"

"She's fine." He smiled. "We have a healthy son. And we are terribly distressed that our dear friend Arn lost his life because of it. I can tell you, officer, that the price we have paid for our happiness is far greater than money or the price of ten trucks."

"My apologies."

"No harm done. I suppose you have to do your job."

"I'm finding out that there are a lot of blue Kenworths out there and a lot of shiny trailers. Is there anything about your truck that would help us identify it? Anything at all?"

"One thing. Come on inside."

Turner led them to a room containing his collection of mounted shift knobs. He had one from each truck he had ever driven, twenty-seven in all, hanging on the wall. They were all the same size, shape and style: about two inches in diameter, finished in chrome with the top side domed to fit the palm of a man's hand. The only difference was that the top of each was engraved with a name, a slogan, and an emblem of some kind. One said 'Desert Storm', another was a copy of Elvis Presley's signature, another engraved with his profile, one even displayed the Harley-Davidson bar and shield emblem.

"The new truck shifter has one word engraved in it: Cary."

"Who's Cary?"

"My baby brother. He died in Desert Storm. I want that truck back, sir."

"Just one more thing. Mr. Perkins' autopsy revealed traces of paraffin on his skin and clothes. Any idea where he might have got that?"

"Paraffin?"

"Wax."

"Oh, sure. We haul produce. Perishable fruit and vegetables. A lot of it is packed in waxed cartons. They hold up better in transit. You see, some states have some pretty rough roads and the load can really get bounced around. Also, it keeps the cartons from soaking up water. Some loads can be vented instead of refrigerated. If your vents are open and you run through rain, water gets in the trailer. If a carton soaks up water, well, I'm sure you can appreciate if you pick up a box of lettuce and the bottom is wet, all the lettuce bounces off your feet because the bottom falls out. The wax keeps that from happening."

"So, how did the wax get on Arnold?"

"This stuff we're talking about is not like car wax, more like candle wax only softer. It rubs off on everything, your clothes, your hands, the inside of your trailer. You have to be inside the trailer to supervise loading and unloading. In fact, sometimes you still have to fingerprint every carton. That shit just rubs off on you every time you touch anything in the trailer. Look, it's why all my clothes are faded. The wife can't wash them in cold water because it sets the wax and they feel all gummy, clammy like. She has to wash them in super hot water to get them clean."

"Fingerprinting cartons?"

"Hand-bombing. Loading or unloading by hand."

"Ahh," said L.T. "You guys still do that?"

"Not because we want to."

"Thanks, Mr. Turner. Good luck with your new baby."

"Find who killed Arn. Find that truck for me."

L.T. had satisfied himself that Gary Turner did not arrange to have his truck stolen to collect the insurance proceeds and was not responsible for the death of Ruby's brother. Suddenly, things looked a little darker for Elvis Wood.

"Where are we going?" Cheryl asked.

"I'm taking you home."

"I'm not ready to go home."

"Good. I could use your help with a couple of things. We're going to Toledo."

The first hour of the ride west was too quiet. Neither spoke, but L.T. sensed something was eating away at Cheryl. Finally, she asked, "Why didn't you come after her?"

"I had no idea where she was."

"I'm not buying that. All these years you've been a policeman. Police find people. It's not like she was hiding."

"I – you have to understand, Cheryl – I was in Viet Nam. I stopped getting letters from her. There was no explanation. Nothing. Four years later I get back and she's been gone for almost as long. Even her folks moved away."

"She was eighteen and pregnant. How could she stay in White Falls?"

"But I didn't know."

"You were just too damn proud, weren't you? You just figured she left you so you were too much a man to go chasing after her. Isn't that right?"

L.T. stared at the road ahead without answering.

"She's been all alone for all these years because you were too damn proud. She pretends to be happy, but all the time it's just like the entertainment business. It's all an act. Never let them know you're hurting. Always make them go away happy."

"But she was married…to that record producer."

"You call that married? Buddy Hart, that major prick. He almost killed her. It's your fault. You should have been there for her."

The conversation ground to a halt as the car traveled on toward Toledo. Cheryl stared out the side window, L.T. watched the road.

Finally, he said, "Cheryl, I…" but the right words seemed elusive.

"It's okay. I'm okay now, Dad. I just had to vent. I suppose I've needed to do that for some time. But I'll be – we'll be fine now." She reached for his hand and held it a long time.

Chapter Fifteen

A little after eleven Sunday night Cheryl checked them into a Best Western in Perrysburg on the west side of Toledo. L.T. wanted to be in Toledo, but figured they had best have a bit more of a cushion between them and White Falls. It was late but he needed to talk with Ruby so he dialed her number at home.

She answered quickly.

"Ruby, I know it's late but –."

"L.T.? Oh, I'm so glad to hear from you. Where the hell have you been? And where are you? Are you okay?"

"I'm fine. What about you?"

The line was silent for a moment, and then she said, "I'm sorry about your apartment. I wish I had been here yesterday when you got home."

"Who was that waitress at the diner? What the hell's going on, Ruby?"

She sighed. "Things are not so good at the diner, L.T. I guess you met Mona."

"Mona? She looks more like an over the hill hooker than a waitress. Where'd you find her?"

"She's okay. A bit pushy, but she's okay. She has experience. She was formerly a cocktail waitress in Atlantic City. You know how hard it is to get good help."

"Priscilla was damn good help."

"Priscilla chose to leave."

Chose to leave? He thought those odd words for Ruby to be using. "Ruby, have you seen two well-dressed guys hanging around town. Have they been in the diner?"

"Yes," she said quietly.

"Were they looking for me?"

"Yes."

"Who are they, Ruby?"

"I don't know," she lied.

"What about this money laundering thing? Are the police charging you?"

"No, that's been all cleared up."

"How?"

"I can't tell you."

"What do you mean you can't tell me? Ruby, what the hell is going on?"

She started to sob and he took a breath. "Oh, L.T., I'm sorry. It's just all so fucked up now." She told him about the deal Ned Dunphy had offered her and how once she agreed her new partners began making changes at the diner. They fired Priscilla and brought in Mona and promised her his apartment. She told him they were taking a big chunk of her revenue off the top and she knew it was only a matter of time before that put her out of business and she would lose everything. She was sobbing uncontrollably now.

"Who's the owner of this PHD Holdings?"

"I don't know, I guess it's those two guys that were looking for you. They're the ones been giving all the orders."

"No, it's not them. They're just somebody's stooges. All right, don't worry about it. I know how to find out. They can't do this to you, Ruby. It's not ethical and it sure as hell isn't legal. I'll get it straightened out. Just don't even whisper my name to anyone right now. You never heard from me."

"Got it." She hung up.

For the first time in months L.T. slept soundly throughout the night. He was awakened at about nine-thirty Monday morning by the ringing of his cell phone.

"Hello."

"Hey, Lover. You sound tired. You weren't out two-timing me last night were you?"

"Ray?"

"Thank the good Lord, the man remembers me."

"I'm not for a minute believing any man could forget you, Ray."

"Flattery will get you anything your heart desires, Lover. Now when are you coming back?"

"I don't know, Ray. I get the feeling you could age me quickly."

"What a way to go."

They both laughed, then Ray said, "Sheriff Henry checked the ranch dwellers. They're a brother and sister that run two trucks in their own outfit called "Sears Refrigerated Transport. Two blue Kenworths and two trailers, one of which is a stainless steel Great Dane."

"And?"

"And the trucks are legal. Pink slips match the VIN plates. Just hard working truckers."

"Any word on my visitors at the Riverside Motel?"

"Those two are connected. They always work as a team, usually on the road. It's like they're traveling enforcers who are rumored to oversee, shall we say, the cleansing of money at remote locations since the tightening of security around casinos."

"That fits. I'm pretty sure they've killed one friend of mine and I'm obviously their next target. Money laundering in White Falls. Who would have guessed?"

"You be careful up there, Lover. Get your narrow ass back down here, I'm craving another look at it."

"Ray, if only I were a decade or so younger."

"Don't you pull that old shit on me, I've road-tested the chassis. Call me soon." She hung up.

He rang up Doobie's cell phone and was surprised to find him at home. "Did your wife sleep on your nightshirt or what?" L.T. asked.

"Horse threw a shoe. I started feeling a vibration on the way to Toronto. It turned out to be the bearing that supports the yoke for the front drive axle. It seized up and spun in the housing. It'll be three or four days before we get a new differential housing so I'm hanging out for this week. Glad to hear you're still in one piece."

"You left too soon. I ran into some old friends, the two who visited me in Dade City."

"Guess you can take care of yourself, eh Stafford."

"I can still hold my own. Call me as soon as you know when you'll be coming this way. I've got more work to do in Florida."

"Thanks, Stafford. It sure is great to have a co-driver I can trust and one that can cover my ass, too." The line went dead.

In a way L.T. was relieved that Doobie wouldn't be along for a week. He didn't relish hiding in Northern Ohio for a week but he liked the idea of being able to get to know Cheryl better. And he needed to check out a couple of things in White Falls. Now he would have time to think and plan his moves carefully.

Marlin was rolling north on I-95 in South Carolina making for Harrisburg, Pennsylvania with a load of tropical plants for a large retail greenhouse complex. The trailer full of plants weighed only about half that of a load of citrus or greens and the Caterpillar engine performed in the Carolina hills like a stallion feeling his oats, chewing up even the steepest of grades without losing speed. The Kenworth soon caught up to a tanker pulled by a laboring Mack Cabover. Marlin checked the mirrors, flipped on the turn signal and flattened the accelerator, wheeling into the left lane. In no time he cruised past the tanker.

"Okay, big truck," called a voice on the CB. "You blew my doors off. Bring it back in."

"Thank you, driver," Marlin replied, and flashed the trailer's marker lights as he pulled back into the right lane.

"You might as well shut down that reefer," said the Mack driver. "You forgot your load back yonder in the Bikini State."

Marlin keyed the mike, laughed and replied, "Not true, driver, I'm loaded. Besides, everyone knows a cat can outrun an old bulldog any day."

"Say what you like, big truck. But I'd bet my speckled pup and my little red wagon you ain't hauling more than twenty bushel. Not much fun when I'm sitting back here dragging fifty."

"Okay, so I'm loaded light. You happy now?"

"Aha. I knew it. What you hauling in that reefer? Another iceman?"

The radio went silent for a moment. Then Marlin spoke. "What the hell is that supposed to mean?"

"Didn't you hear about that poor slob freight hauler they found frozen stiff up in the Buckeye?"

"Of course."

"They figure some pilled-up reefer jockey, some produce hauler, iced him and dumped him there."

"So?"

"So, it's easy to see you ain't hauling much. Maybe all you got in there is a big old Popsicle that once upon a time was a freight driver."

"That's ridiculous."

"Aw, relax driver. I'm just having fun with you. Say, did you hear they found another one this morning?"

"Another what?" Marlin asked.

"Another frozen trucker? Found him on a hillside along a skinny road just off the Interstate near London, Kentucky."

"No," Marlin replied. "No, what did you hear?"

"Not much, really. They was talking it up back there at the truck stop in Brunswick. Didn't know who the dude was yet but somebody reported seeing a blue KW and a reefer get off that exit last night some time. Truck sounds a might familiar, don't it?"

"Yeah," said Marlin. "Damn glad I haven't been to Kentucky lately."

"Right. Any more in your outfit look like that?"

"No," he lied. "There's only me. I'm just a lone independent, a short, fat, handsome truck driver come movie star."

"Guess we're safe then," said the other driver, and the radio went quiet.

179

Marlin glanced over at the passenger seat.

Mickey: "She's at it again."

Marlin: "Can't be her."

Mickey: "Oh, really? Where is she?"

Marlin: "On her way to the Motor City. Up I-75."

Mickey: "What Interstate runs right past London, Kentucky?"

Marlin: "Okay, but why?"

Mickey: "What the hell am I, a shrink? The bitch is spun. She's on overload, you said it yourself. She love's killing guys, man. Probably fucks them silly first, right there in the reefer. Probably getting her nut off in there. Guy nods off in the afterglow, wakes up freezing and can't get out. Dead in a couple hours, maybe less in one of these babies."

Marlin: "That fucking bitch."

Mickey: "I told you, man, she gets off on it. She's not going to stop until somebody stops her. She's on one fucking power trip."

Marlin: "I know that. That's why she's doing it. To have it over me. Ever since that night in Wildwood at the truck stop, she's had it over me. I'll just show her again, anybody can play her game. Only I'll be the winner."

Mickey: "And just how do you expect to do that?"

Marlin: "Simple. I'll freeze somebody too."

Mickey: "Freeze? You're going to freeze some shitbag in the reefer? Give your head a shake. That's why she's got it over you, man."

Marlin: "What the hell you talking about?"

Mickey: "I'm talking about freezing somebody is chickenshit. Just like making a car fall off a jack and squashing a guy like a cockroach is pure chickenshit.

180

You haven't got the guts to really kill somebody the way that pretty young thing did for you. She ran that screwdriver clean through that driver to save your sorry ass. She iced him one-on-one by hand, not by ramming his car."

Marlin: "Dead is dead. What's the difference if you freeze them or stab them? They're still dead."

Mickey: "You can't do it, can you? You haven't got the balls to stand face-to-face with some dude and just pull the trigger."

Marlin stared at the passenger seat too long and the truck's right wheels slipped onto the rumble strip on the edge of the pavement causing the large radial tires to sing out fiercely. He looked ahead and wheeled the Kenworth back into the right lane. The trailer followed, swaying on its air-ride suspension.

Mickey: "You really can't do it, can you? Look, it's just not that difficult. I've done it dozens of times."

Marlin: "Eat shit, Mickey. We're not talking about the movies. Get your head out of your ass."

Mickey: "Me? What about you? Tell me something, ace. When you shut down the dude in the Beemer how did you feel?"

Marlin: "What's that got to do with it?"

Mickey: "Got everything to do with it, driver. Felt good, didn't you?"

Marlin: "Okay."

Mickey: "Felt major fucking adrenaline, didn't you? Felt powerful, didn't you? Huh? Didn't you?"

Marlin: "Okay. It felt good. It felt damn good."

Mickey: "Oh yeah. Do the next one with that dude's nickel-plated revolver. Just walk up to some shitbag and blast holes in him. Now that feels a hundred times better than what you felt on that hillside in Georgia. I guarantee, you look him in the eye when you do it, you'll feel a hundred times better than that whacked out sister of yours. Then, and only then, will she realize that she can never top you. Then, and only then, will you have power over her. That kind of power is everlasting."

Marlin stared straight ahead now. The cab grew quiet but for the drone of the engine and the whine of the tires. His hands gripped the Kenworth's large leather-covered steering wheel and twisted and twisted without turning the wheel. He knew what he had to do and he couldn't stop thinking about it.

Marlin pulled into a truckstop in Baltimore an hour and a half from Harrisburg. It was nine-thirty in the evening. He would deliver the plants first thing in the morning, then head for a chemical plant near Kanauga, Ohio where he would load vats of insecticide for the Port of Miami. There, the containers of bug spray would be transferred to a ship bound for Argentina. It was an easy haul-back that paid well. If all went as planned he would offload in Miami Friday and be back at the ranch for supper. First, though, there remained some very important business to tend to.

He grabbed a shower at the truck stop and went into the drivers' lounge to catch the news. There was no mention of any "iceman" killing so Marlin asked a couple of other drivers in the lounge if they had heard about it.

"Yeah," said an overweight man in khaki pants and shirt with a "UPS" crest. "That story about a frozen driver in Kentucky was bullshit, man. Some fisherman fell out of a boat in that lake alongside I-75. He didn't freeze to death; he drowned. Wasn't no iceman."

"Are you sure?"

"Positive. Our trucks cover I-75 twenty-four/seven. We get the news before the TV gets it. Hell, we get it before the Highway Patrol."

Marlin shuffled out of the lounge past a state trooper who had just stopped in for coffee. He made his way back to his truck. So Carla hadn't done it after all. He had parked in the back row of the parking lot where he could think and plan. The adrenaline surge caused by his decision to kill again had kept him in the can for a half hour with his bowels churning. Now, it was all for nothing. Carla hadn't killed again, as earlier believed.

All afternoon and evening he could concentrate on nothing else. Carla had to be put in her place or he would never have control. Suddenly he realized that had not changed. She still felt she was in control of the company and in control of him. To restore himself to his rightful position of honor and control he must kill someone. And not by freezing. It had to be swift, powerful and violent or neither Carla nor Mickey would respect him, ever. And it couldn't be just anyone, it had to be someone important.

Trooper Calvin Miles of the Maryland Highway Patrol slid onto a stool at the truckstop. Sarah smoothed the skirt of her uniform, winked at him, and brought him a steaming cup of coffee.

"Hey, Captain Calvin."

He grinned and blushed. "Hey, Sarah. And it's Trooper, not Captain."

She leaned on the counter smiling. "So modest," she teased. "Catching any bad dudes tonight?"

"Pretty quiet so far."

"So are you. What's it going to take for me to get you out of your shell?"

He shook his head. "Don't pull that on me, Sarah. You know I'm happily married."

"Oh sure," she said. "I'd just like you to be happily fooling around, is all."

He looked around to make certain no one was within earshot then leaned over and quietly said, "I just couldn't do that to my wife."

Sarah unfastened an extra button on her blouse and leaned over a little farther to show him more of her firm, round breasts. She whispered in his ear, "I don't want you to do it to your wife. I want you to do it to me, silly."

He turned a deeper shade of red and took a sip of his coffee. She reached over and felt his bicep.

"Damn, I bet you're a powerful man. Want to handcuff me?"

He sputtered, nearly choking on his coffee as he felt his jockey shorts tightening. His hand began to shake so he put down his cup but didn't say anything.

Sarah was still leaning close to him, her hot breath gently caressing and warming his cheeks.

"Sure would like to get a peek at your nightstick," she said, looking him square in the eyes.

A crackly voice came over his portable a bit too loud and he jumped, then grinned and turned it down a bit. His thumb squeezed the microphone button on his shoulder and as he bowed his head to speak into it his hair brushed hers and he stiffened in his seat. His voice quivered as he acknowledged the call and indicated he would respond.

The female dispatcher relayed the report of a naked woman wandering in the back row of the truck parking lot. She asked if he wanted backup. The trooper was up from his seat and out the door before Sarah could button her blouse.

"So that's it," she said to herself. "I've got to get naked for him to make a move."

Trooper Miles cruised very slowly toward the far reaches of the parking lot, stopping his patrol car briefly to peer between rows of tractor-trailer rigs. He turned into the back row and stopped but saw no sign of anyone, especially a naked woman. He urged the car forward at a crawl, past a blue Kenworth with a reefer, shining a hand-held spotlight between each pair of trucks. About a third of the way down the row his foot hit the brake pedal sharply when he spied a piece of white clothing on the asphalt between two trailers. He stepped out of the car with his flashlight held up near eye level and crept between the trailers. Kneeling down, he picked up the cloth and examined it with his flashlight. It turned out to be a pair of men's boxer shorts. He dropped them, stood and turned to head back to his car and took a thirty-eight caliber bullet in the forehead.

Marlin eased the Kenworth out of the parking lot and headed for Harrisburg. Once on the highway, he mashed the accelerator and the twin chrome stacks belched black smoke over the trailer, the Caterpillar powerhouse roaring. He had decided not to spend the night at the truckstop in Baltimore but to get as far away as he could before the dead trooper was found. He hadn't bought any fuel at the stop and hadn't used a credit card for his meal so there was no physical record of him being there.

He could have stayed. He could have played it cool and made a statement that he was awakened by the sound of a gunshot but he thought better of having his name on record as being present at the scene of the murder. So he pounded the highway north for Harrisburg, his body on fire and quaking all over at the sheer power he possessed. Twice he reached for the pocket of his jeans to make sure the officer's badge was still there. Mickey didn't say a word but Marlin knew he was smiling the whole time.

Chapter Sixteen

For the most part, L.T. and his daughter spent a quiet week getting to know each other and even doing a bit of sightseeing. On Wednesday he bought an Indians baseball cap, sunglasses and a shoulder-length reddish wig and he and Cheryl drove to White Falls. He showed her around, pointing out the homes of both grandparents and the high school that he and Natalie attended. Then they parked across the street from the Savings and Loan. His idea was to tail Claire Mackie, the teller with assets beyond her means. But the more he thought it through, the less sense it made that she was embezzling. Morgan and Gambino were enforcers for the outfit in Atlantic City. They were too heavily connected to be dealing with an employee. Whatever was going on in that bank was coming from the top down. Claire Mackie was not the one he needed to squeeze. They headed back to the motel where he could plan his next move.

Thursday afternoon Doobie called to say the Freightliner was almost ready and he'd be making his regular run on Monday. He told L.T. to be ready early Monday afternoon and to be geared up to drive because the wife had been screwing him silly and he would need to spend some serious time in the sleeper. L.T. called Ray to let her know he'd be back down sometime Tuesday.

L.T. was getting restless. He had been in hiding with his daughter nearly a week and while he delighted at having new-found family he felt he needed a little space. Or maybe he needed work. The feeling that he was trapped in a situation that kept him very unproductive had been creeping up on him. There was this growing feeling that he had let Ruby down by not being able to help her out of her jam. The fact that he was getting nowhere at finding her brother's killer served to pull him even lower and had him precariously close to sinking into a sea of self-doubt. He had studied his notes every chance he got, but something was missing. He didn't know why, though he felt that that missing piece was in Florida. Doobie wouldn't be back until Monday and cash was running short so he was stuck in Ohio for a few days. Something had to break loose and he had to make it happen.

Late Friday night L.T. slipped out of the room and into Cheryl's rented car but the keys were nowhere to be found. He knocked softly on her door. She peeked out between the curtains then switched the light on and let him in. "Did you miss me?" she asked.

"I'm sorry to wake you, Cheryl, but I need the keys to your car."

"Where are you going?"

"I've got to run over to White Falls and have a chat with someone."

"It's dangerous for you there."

"I'll be careful."

She pulled the keys from her purse but didn't give them to him. Instead she snatched up her jeans and shirt and went into the bathroom.

"Cheryl, what are you doing? I need the keys," he said to the bathroom door.

"I'm going with you. I'll be out in a minute."

"No, Cheryl. You said it yourself, it's dangerous."

"That's right. I finally get the courage to meet you and now you think you can just walk out of my life by getting yourself killed? No way, I'm going to protect you."

His brow wrinkled. She came out the door, slipped into her shoes and said, "So, you ready or what?"

He followed her to the car. They made one stop at the Flying J Truck Plaza and L.T. went inside. He returned momentarily with a small sack in one hand, a very large one in the other. He laid the large sack on the floor in the back seat. It made a clanking sound that surprised Cheryl. When he climbed back in the front he handed the small sack to Cheryl and drove out onto the highway heading for White Falls.

"Fix this up for me, will you?" He pointed to the sack. "Man, they sell everything in a truck stop. Everything." He was smiling.

Cheryl pulled a micro cassette recorder and package of batteries from the sack. In a moment she had it assembled, and said, "Okay, what do I do with it now?"

"Test it."

She switched it on and sang a few bars of one of her mother's hits. L.T.'s eyes began to water. He couldn't get over how she was so much like Natalie. Her voice gave him goose bumps, it's softness felt like velvet on his skin.

"Well, what do you think?"

"Quit your day job immediately, you're going to be a star."

She beamed.

"This gives me an idea," he said, and explained his plan.

Cheryl opened the cell phone and punched in the number. A groggy-sounding voice answered after the fourth ring.

"Is this Mr. Dunphy?"

"Yes. Who is this?"

"Mr. Dunphy, you probably don't remember me but I'm Natalie Pearson."

"Who?"

"You'll probably recognize me as Nat Pearce, the Nashville Nightingale."

"Sure."

"No really. Listen, I just finished a show in Detroit and I'm driving to Cleveland to do another tomorrow. You can probably tell I'm on a cell phone on the road right now."

"You sound like her. What do you want?"

"Mr. Dunphy, I'm not sure if you remember but I was born and raised in White Falls."

"Of course, everyone knows that." He was beginning to perk up now.

"You may not know it but I've made a lot of money over the years."

"I can appreciate that, Ms. Pearce."

"Well, as you know, investment markets have not been favorable of late so I've been seeking some alternative means of growing my capital and I thought, 'Wouldn't it be great if I could invest some money in my old home town of White Falls and maybe return there to retire one day.' You see?"

"Go on." He was sounding interested now.

"So I talked to an advisor in Nashville and he punched up his computer and looked in White Falls and says, 'Ned Dunphy. He's the man to see in Northern Ohio'."

"Really?"

"I swear. Well, you know how difficult it is to get a minute to yourself in the entertainment business so, the best I could do was to rent a car and drive here on my way to Cleveland in hopes of catching a few moments with you to chat about investment ideas. I'm sure it could prove very lucrative for you. Could you please spare me just a few minutes?"

"All right, I suppose I can meet with you. Name the place."

"Oh, I can't be seen in public with a strange man in the middle of the night. You know how that is. My advisor gave me your address, I'll just meet you there."

"Okay. I suppose that's okay."

"And Mr. Dunphy. Please don't have any lights on. I can't risk being seen here. I have my career to think about. You know what the public is like when you're famous."

"Sure," he said. "When will you be here?"

"I'm on your front porch right now." She hung up. In a few moments the door opened and a bald man in a robe appeared. He opened his mouth to speak but before he could a large hand clamped over it from the side and he was led mumbling and wriggling to a car.

"What's shaking, Dumpy?" said L.T. "Glad to see me?" He tossed the man into the trunk and slammed the lid. They drove quickly out of town and caught 412 to the bridge that crosses the Sandusky River. When he spotted the laneway L.T. turned off the highway and followed the narrow dirt path to a spot on the bank just under the bridge. L.T. took the large sack and pulled a long length of chain from it. He walked out from under the bridge and tossed one end around a tree limb about eight feet off the ground and let both ends dangle. He walked back and opened the trunk.

Ned Dunphy was curled up in a fetal position, cowering and shaking under the trunk light.

"You make a sound," said L.T., and smashed the trunk light bulb with his fist. "This is what I do to you."

Dunphy moaned as bits of glass fell on him. L.T.'s large hands dragged him from the trunk and straight over to the chain. Just enough moonlight filtered through the trees and reflected off the water to light the shiny chain links hanging ominously from the black branch.

"You see this?" He took a length of chain in his hand and wrapped it about the bald man's neck. The cold steel made him shake and quake and he couldn't stop his bladder from emptying itself down his legs and onto his bare feet. "This is a mechanical necktie just like the one somebody wrapped around Kendall Griffith the night he drew his last breath. I know his partners did it. I know you know who they are. You are now going to tell me who they are." His hands gripped the other end of the chain and pulled it taut. Dunphy's head jerked upward. The tension of the chain elicited a muffled scream from the wide-eyed bald man in the bathrobe.

"I don't know," he choked out the words.

L.T. slowly raised the chain, lifting the man onto his tiptoes and shutting off his airway totally. The color drained from him and his eyes bulged. Cheryl leaned against the car, watching intently.

L.T. lowered the man again, loosened the necktie and said, "Who's muscling Ruby? Who's been looking for me?"

"You're going to be in a lot of trouble when Chief Mackenzie finds out about this," the man whined.

"For your information, Dumpy, I am already aware that Chief Mackenzie is as crooked as a corkscrew and is involved in your little money-laundering con job."

L.T. dragged the chain off the limb, removed it from Dunphy's neck and led him over to the riverbank. He knelt down and wrapped the cold steel around the man's ankles, stood up and pushed him hard into the chill waters of the Sandusky.

"Dad!" Cheryl called out as she heard the splash, watched the man disappear beneath the murky surface.

L.T. waited a moment, and then hauled in his catch. Dunphy coughed and gasped and sputtered on the bank. His captor raised him up and led him back under the tree, wrapped the chain about his neck again and tossed the other end over the limb.

"Now, let's make the necktie a little tighter, like your boys did with Kendall." He grabbed the chain.

"Wait," said Dunphy. "I can't take any more. You're right. It's PHD Holdings. That's the name of the company."

"Who's the boss?"

"We're partners, the four of us. But Orville runs things."

"Hennessey?"

He nodded, shaking uncontrollably. "PHD, for Pruitt, Hennessey, and Dunphy."

"Randy's in this too?" He laughed. "Oh, this is too good to be true. And Mackenzie is the fourth? How come it's not PHDM?"

"You know how Pruitt is about smart things. He figures PHD makes him sound smart. Man has an ego the size of Lake Erie. Smart my ass. Besides, Mackenzie came along later. We needed someone with the police to allow us to work without fear of investigation and capture."

"But Mackenzie came on ten years ago. Matter of fact it was just after Chief Paetz had his accident and died from being thrown off a horse and busting his head. You bastards killed him." L.T. was beginning to shake with rage and Dunphy could see it in his fiery eyes.

"It wasn't me, L.T. You've got to believe me. The money was just starting to flow. We had acquired silent partnerships in several businesses around town and we were making it, finally. Willard Paetz started checking into things, nosing around in our business. Hennessey is ruthless. He wasn't about to risk what we had built up. He said we had to protect ourselves."

"That night," L.T. thought aloud. I was supposed to ride with the Chief the morning he died but the night before I ran into Natalie."

Cheryl's head cocked to one side and she slowly walked over from the car, listening intently now.

"So, you're saying Natalie was in on this?" L.T. asked.

"No. That was pure serendipity. We knew you were going to be with the Chief that morning. You were to meet a similar fate. But when your wife found you in that motel with Natalie we knew you were ruined."

"You fucking slime bag," he raised an arm to backhand him but changed his mind and kicked him in the groin. The fat man's knees buckled and he groaned.

"Those guys that came looking for me. They killed Kendall?"

"And Paetz."

"Who are they?"

"Morgan and Gambino. They're from Atlantic City. They do us favors from time to time because we run some of their drug money through our businesses to clean it up."

L.T. took the chain off Dunphy's neck and put him back in the trunk of the car. "Let's get out of here," he said to Cheryl.

"You were with my mother in White Falls ten years ago? You spent a night with her in a motel?"

"Just long enough to wreck a marriage and a career."

"Don't blame my mother for your troubles."

"I'm not. It was the best night of my life."

They drove toward Toledo. L.T. called Chester Connor, a friend with the Ohio State Patrol, apologized for rousing him and arranged for them to meet at the Waffle House near the Airport exit of I-475. In an hour they pulled in. The only other car was Connor's patrol car.

The two men shook hands and L.T. introduced Cheryl.

"I never knew you had family," said Connor.

L.T. smiled. "I see they trust you with a car now."

"Parking lot's getting too small. They figure it won't get banged up at my place. What's up?"

They entered the restaurant and ordered coffee. L.T. played the tape of the conversation of him and Dunphy at the river.

"Jesus," Connor said, shaking his head. "We're talking major scandal here. But you know, I always thought that something was not right with that Mackenzie. Jesus. Of course, you realize that tape will not be admissible in court."

"Of course. But it's damn sure enough to get an investigation going. You've got names, dates, and murder one. Twice. Besides, I can get you a statement directly from the guy on the tape."

"How?"

"Follow me." L.T led him out to the rear of the car and opened the trunk.

"Jesus. How am I supposed to take him in looking like this?"

"Just tell them you found him wandering drunk."

They put the still wet and shivering Ned Dunphy in the back of the patrol car. Cheryl brought him a cup of steaming coffee. "You really look like Natalie," he said.

"One more thing," L.T. said to Connor. "You know anything about this frozen stiff they pulled out of Hennessey's place?"

"I was there. Guy's a trucker from Oklahoma. M.E. said he died of severe hypothermia. He actually froze to death. We were stumped at first as to how that might happen. We had originally thought somebody killed him and stuffed him in a freezer to keep for a while but no. He hadn't even been reported missing. His wife

196

said he was on his regular run to Cleveland. Last seen in a bar there. Left with a knockout in a tight red dress. Sounds like a hooker. No signs of trauma except for a couple of broken fingernails. I mean, this one was weird. We had no idea but the M.E. reports finding paraffin and this composite material under his fingernails. We go to the FBI with samples and they come back in short order saying the paraffin was some low-grade wax, nothing there. But the composite material was this insulation that they use to line refrigerated truck trailers." He checked his notes. "Specifically, those trailers manufactured by Dorsey and Great Dane."

L.T.'s eyes widened. He jotted a couple of notes in his book.

"What," said Connor. "What is it?"

"Truck trailers. And paraffin. I'm working on something similar in Florida."

"A frozen stiff in Florida?"

"No. But paraffin and trucks are definitely involved. Could you check with your FBI contact and see if anything comes up in the VICAP system?"

"Can't you?"

"No."

"Why not?"

"You know the guy named Pruitt, the one implicated on the tape?"

"The mayor?"

"I lost my job last week for knocking out a couple of his teeth."

Connor laughed. "Looks like you're about to be reinstated, my friend."

Chapter Seventeen

Doobie picked them up at the motel in Perrysburg about suppertime Monday. Cheryl insisted on riding in the truck with him, saying she could not bear to let him out of her sight. He finally agreed on the condition that she only ride as far as Tennessee. Doobie said it was no big deal to pick up I-71 in Kentucky, run it over to I-65 south through Louisville and down to Nashville, drop her off and grab I-24 over to I-75 south at Chattanooga. Cheryl knuckled under, but wished he would take her to Florida with him.

To Cheryl's total surprise, Doobie tossed the keys to L.T. and he climbed in behind the wheel. Doobie helped Cheryl up and in, and then gave her the buddy seat while he sat in the sleeper compartment.

"Oh my God," she said. "You're actually going to drive this thing? You know how?"

He winked at her, pushed the clutch all the way to the floor, slipped the stick into gear and massaged Dolly Parton's breasts in different directions. The massive rig, with its load of steel RV frames stacked high and held in place with long chains and binders, eased forward smoothly and rolled onto the highway with black smoke blowing. Cheryl sat speechless in total admiration of the man. Doobie grinned from ear to ear and said, "I taught him, eh."

L.T. felt very settled behind the wheel of Doobie's eighteen-wheeler and that worried him. Never in his life had he considered a career as a truck driver, but he had to admit to himself that it was feeling good, damn good. He was cruising past Wapakoneta on I-75 when his cell phone rang. He lifted his free hand from its rest on the shift lever and pulled the phone from his shirt pocket.

"This is L.T."

"It's Connor. You sound like you're in your car."

"That's an understatement. How are things in White Falls."

"Under investigation, but that's not why I called. I found out something very interesting when I ran your idea of trucks and paraffin through the VICAP system. Came up with two hits. Two very surprising hits."

L.T. fished out his notepad and pencil and handed them to Cheryl. He repeated aloud to her the words spoken by Trooper Connor. "A trucker named Arnold Perkins murdered in Florida was found to have traces of paraffin on his clothing and person. He was alleged to have been stabbed at a truckstop in Wildwood where, coincidentally was found a thirty-eight caliber slug. This particular slug matched perfectly one taken from the body of Maryland State Trooper Calvin Miles who was killed last week in a truckstop in Baltimore by assailants unknown."

"Guess that means we're heading in the right direction." He hung up.

The next morning they bid a tearful goodbye at the truck stop at Nashville. Cheryl had begged him to let her call her mother to meet them for breakfast but L.T. said he wouldn't have a reunion in a truck stop. Doobie asked why the hell not and L.T. told him to shut up.

Marlin was shocked at the change in Carla. His plan had come through. She seemed to be in awe when he showed her the badge of the murdered Maryland Trooper and was finally back to her old sweet self. He couldn't believe it when it came time to head for Belle Glade and pick up their loads Tuesday morning.

Carla said, "I've made a decision, Fish. Since you run this company and I work for you, you should have the new rig like we originally planned. I don't feel right driving it because I know it belongs to you. I want my old truck back."

"Well, well. I'm glad to see you've finally come to your senses, little sister."

The next morning L.T. and Doobie arrived in Jacksonville and watched as a special crane at the RV manufacturing plant offloaded the frames. Next, they rolled on down to Wildwood where Doobie intended to spend the night before going on to Naples in the morning for another load of Cypress mulch. They climbed down from the rig at the Wildwood truck stop and L.T. was about to call Ray White when a blue Mercedes with tinted windows pulled up beside them. Cheryl's head popped up through the open sunroof.

"Need a lift, Mister?" she asked.

L.T. shook his head. "You're not here, Cheryl."

"Cut the crap, Dad. I've been driving all day and I'm tired. You're here to investigate and you need wheels. I'm here to protect you and I have wheels. You don't take me with you, I just keep following."

Doobie looked at L.T. and said, "She's got you by the ass, eh."

"Eh," said L.T.

Doobie shook his hand again and said, "I'll be back through tomorrow afternoon. You know how to reach me if you need a ride home. Looks like you're in pretty good hands, though."

L.T.'s cell phone was ringing in his pocket. He waved to Doobie and answered it.

"Thought you should know the FBI is involved in the Perkins homicide investigation now," said Trooper Trout.

"Now that would be because of the Trooper shot at a truckstop in Baltimore," said L.T.

"You know about that?"

"I ran into a friend with the Ohio State Patrol who's been working on the iceman murder up there. It may be tied to this also."

"Now that is weird."

"L.T. drove toward Zephyrhills while Cheryl spent the time browsing through his notes and asking the odd question.

"What's the dog got to do with it?" she asked.

"Dog? What dog?"

"The Great Dane?"

"No, that's not a dog it's a brand of truck trailer." He stared at her a moment. "Hey, that could be it. I think you've got it. That could be the connection."

"What connection?"

"What kind of trailer did Gary Turner own?"

She flipped pages back. "A stainless steel Great Dane."

"What kind of trailer did Elvis Wood say dumped the body off the bridge?"

"Big, shiny motherfucker. Great Dane."

"What kind of trailer did Connor say had that composite they found under the iceman's fingernails?"

"Dorsey and Great Dane."

"That's the connection. One thing I've noticed: most of the van type trailers out here, whether refrigerated or not, are painted white. Not many are big, shiny motherfuckers. There are a lot of blue Kenworths. But there can't be many blue Kenworths pulling stainless steel Great Dane trailers. It's got to be that pair with the ranch."

"But it says here that the Sheriff of Pasco County checked their trucks and they were not stolen."

"It's just too coincidental that these people reported by Wood to have dumped the body, have an exact duplicate of Turner's truck. It has to be them. Nice going, Cheryl. Let's see if we can find it."

She beamed.

L.T. slowed down. "What's that coming out of the driveway up ahead? That's the entrance to the ranch."

"What ranch?" Cheryl asked.

"The one Elvis said the killer went to after he dumped the body."

"And that's a big, blue truck pulling a shiny trailer."

The rig rolled slowly toward them, its sandy-haired driver working it through the gears. They slowed and spotted the red K on the grill, turned toward each other and said in unison, "Kenworth." As the trailer passed them, L.T. made a quick U-turn and pulled in behind the shiny trailer to follow. They caught the name plate on the lower left corner of the left barn door. "Great Dane," they both said at once.

They followed the truck at a safe distance up through Dade City, across the US98 Bridge and onto I-75 north. A half hour later they watched the man wheel the rig into the truck stop at Wildwood. L.T. followed. The big rig circled the restaurant and came up on the west side of the building and rolled to a hissing stop at the fuel pumps. The driver got out, held two thumbs up at the black fuel attendant and sauntered toward the entrance to the Truckers' Store. L.T. parked near the restaurant and waited for the man to go inside the store. He got out and told Cheryl to wait while he walked over to the truck.

"Can I help you sir?"

"No, thank you," said L.T, raising his voice over the roar of the diesel refrigeration unit. "I just saw this beautiful truck and I thought I would have a look at it. Do you think the driver would mind if I climbed up there and just peeked in the window?"

"Well, most drivers pretty particular about them rigs. But I ain't gonna tell."

L.T. thanked him and climbed up on the tank step and peered inside. He tried to see if the shift knob was engraved but the tint on the side window was just too dark. He couldn't make it out. He climbed down and went back to the car.

"Well?" asked Cheryl.

"Windows are tinted. Couldn't tell."

"Let me try," she said, reaching for the door handle.

"No. You stay here, I'll take another look."

He wandered back to the truck but again couldn't quite see the shift knob. Frustrated, he headed back to the car. Cheryl was not in the car and nowhere in sight.

He went inside and looked around for her. He checked the restaurant, and then waited outside the door to the ladies' room. A few minutes passed, but no Cheryl. He checked the car again. She was not there but the blue Kenworth with the shiny Great Dane had pulled out and was just taking the ramp to I-75 north. L.T. went back inside and described Cheryl to the woman at the fuel desk.

"That sounds like the pretty young thing just left with Fish."

"Fish?"

"Young guy, kind of quiet. Drives a blue Kenworth."

L.T. was out the door and on the road with tires squealing. He caught up with the rig as it exited the Belleview scale about ten miles north of Wildwood. The sun was setting as L.T. pulled up alongside the Kenworth and blew the horn. He waved frantically at the truck's driver who opened the window and gave him the finger.

"Pull over," said L.T.

"Fuck you, asshole."

"Please, it's important," L.T. shouted. "I don't want any trouble."

"What do you want?"

A blast from an air horn caused L.T. to look back at the road to find the Mercedes half in the center lane, half in the far left. A Peterbilt pulling a tanker full of orange juice concentrate was trying to pass on the left with L.T. in the way. The Mercedes swerved to the right to avoid the tanker, the Kenworth swerved onto the shoulder to avoid the Mercedes and finally pulled to a stop to see if any damage was done. L.T. wheeled the car to a stop just ahead of the truck and jumped out. He ran to the passenger door of the rig and climbed up on the step but Cheryl was not in the seat. He tugged the door open and looked in. No sign of her.

"What the hell's going on, mister?"

"At the truck stop they said my daughter left with you."

"Oh, she's your daughter? What's her name, Cheryl? Nice young woman. Asked to have a look inside a big truck. They don't come any bigger than this so I showed her around and she left."

"What's back there?" L.T. asked, motioning toward the sleeper.

"That's my rolling motel room." He paused waiting for the stranger to speak again but he didn't so the driver said, "Come on in and have a look."

"Thanks," said L.T. and hauled himself in over the seat and into the sleeper. To his surprise she was not there. "Sorry, driver. I can't imagine where she went."

"I'd like to help, mister but I've got to haul my load up north. Maybe you should haul yours back to the truck stop. She's probably in the bathroom."

"Thanks again," he said, and on his way out he noticed the name 'Cary' etched into the top of the shifter handle. As he stepped outside the reefer engine picked up speed. L.T.'s feet had barely touched the ground when the truck lurched backward with a roar. L.T. ran after it, jumped on the driver's side step and shouted through the window, "Show me what's in the trailer."

The truck lurched violently as the driver slammed on the brakes. At the same time he reached out and pushed hard against L.T.'s chest, who tumbled roughly to the ground and had to roll out of the way of the trailer wheels as the truck shot forward and turned out onto the highway. He ran for his car and followed, fumbling to punch numbers into his cell phone. He called *FHP, the emergency number for the Highway Patrol.

"911 emergency service. Please state your name and the nature of your emergency."

"Sergeant L.T. Stafford of the White Falls Police Department in Ohio. I'm following a murder suspect northbound on I-75. He's in a stolen tractor-trailer rig, Florida tag number seven-two-two-Tom-Adam-four-three."

"One moment please."

He waited.

"I'm sorry, sir. That vehicle is not reported stolen."

"Then someone has switched the tags, ma'am. Use your head."

"Try to stay calm, sir. What is your location?"

"I just passed mile marker three-one-two. Can you get somebody out here to stop this truck immediately?"

"Sir, you say you think the driver is a murder suspect?"

"Yes."

"You have reason to believe this person murdered whom?"

"Arnold Perkins, the trucker they pulled out of the Withlacoochee River near Dade City a week ago."

"I'm afraid that's impossible sir, the suspect in that case has already been apprehended."

"Look, lady this guy has my daughter in his trailer and if we don't stop him he's going to freeze her to death."

"Okay sir, we read the papers too. We'll send someone to investigate as soon as we have an officer free but it may take a while. Have a nice day." The line went dead.

He punched in Doobie's number. It took about five rings for him to answer.

"Where the hell are you?"

"I'm in the can." L.T. heard a toilet flush. "This constipation is a bitch, eh."

"Haul ass north on I-75. I'm following this crazy trucker and he's got Cheryl in the trailer with the reefer running."

"Holy shit, I'm on it. How far north are you?"

"Mile three-two-one running about sixty-five."

"I'll haul ass but you better try to slow him down, it'll take me an hour to make up twenty miles."

L.T. hung up and pulled out to pass the Kenworth. As he drew alongside the rig began inching left across the line and into his lane. L.T. eased the Mercedes into the left lane but the big rig kept coming so he braked and fell in behind again. He slowed to see if the driver of the truck would do the same but he wasn't buying any of that. He couldn't help wondering just how cold it was getting inside that trailer.

The pair kept jousting. L.T. tried passing left, then right, and so on. Whenever they crossed lanes the traffic around them would blast horns and wave fists or fingers. Once L.T. swung the Mercedes into the left lane to take the middle spot in a line of five cars passing. The trucker didn't change his strategy, just bore left and ran all five into the grassy median. L.T. hoped someone would call in a description to the FHP to help corroborate his statement.

It was dark by the time Doobie's marker lights made the Freightliner's grille loom large in his rear view mirror. L.T. swung left and the silver truck pulled up along side, Doobie's head out the window. "You want to pull over and get in with me?" he called down to the open sunroof.

"No time for that. Move into the center lane and hold it steady. I'll come up on the right."

The Mercedes backed off and Doobie swung the rig into the middle lane. L.T. drew alongside and adjusted the cruise control until the car matched the pace of the truck. He raised himself up to sit on the top of the seatback, leaning one arm in to hold the wheel steady. Next, he boosted himself up and sat on the roof with his right foot on the wheel, the other leg dangling over the driver's door. The car's steering was touchy and he found it extremely difficult to control it with his foot. The car weaved left and right, swerving and bumping Doobie's truck with sparks showering the road behind, then back to the right and away. Traffic behind backed off when the fire started flying. L.T. readied himself for transfer to the truck and tried to ease the car to the left again. He got both hands up and the left leg out ready to go for the grab handle on the side of the cab but the car came left too sharply and he had to lift his leg out of the way to keep from pinning it as the car struck the truck again.

L.T. took a breath and went for it one more time. This time as the car slammed against the truck he took his foot off the wheel and leaped up for the grab handle. He clutched it with his left, the right missed and as the car moved away to the right his foot caught on the edge of the open sunroof and he found himself being stretched in a prone position over unforgiving asphalt at a deadly speed. He made an effort to straighten his foot and at the same time got his right hand on the grab handle. The foot sprung free and his legs fell suddenly, his feet rubbing the pavement and starting to burn but he managed to hang on. In a moment he was sitting in the passenger seat working frantically to remove his smoldering shoes. He glanced out the window in time to see the car trail off the right shoulder, through a fence and crash violently into a grove of pines, exploding in an orange ball of flaming gasoline.

"Nice of you to drop by, L.T."

He tossed the shoes and socks out the window and frowned at his friend.

"So, what's the plan? You want me to run him off the road, get in front and hit the brakes, what? Lucky thing we're empty, we can run like the wind and stop on a dime."

"We're not going to fuck with this asshole. He's psychotic. He'll just ram hell out of us and keep going. I believe he'd wreck that thing to keep us from getting him. And I can't risk that. I'm going out. You get me close. When I signal, hit the brakes."

"Hard?"

"No. Real fucking hard. Now fall in behind him and douse the lights." L.T. slipped out the door, made his way along the top of the fuel tank and around the fiery exhaust stack to the catwalk behind the cab. He reached up on the headache rack and came down with a thirty-six foot length of steel chain with a hook on each end used to go all the way over the stacks of RV frames and hook onto both sides of the flatbed trailer.

He knelt down and struggled in the darkness to wrap the end of the chain around the truck's frame and the I-beam brace of the exhaust stack. Twice he burned his hands on the searing pipe but he never said a word. Once satisfied the chain was securely anchored, he made his way back along the side carrying the coils of heavy steel on one arm. He tossed the mass of chain onto the truck's fiberglass hood and caught Doobie raising a hand to his face in horror. L.T. leapt onto the hood, grabbed the chain and pulled the anchored end taught to brace himself as Doobie eased down on the accelerator. The engine roared and the wind whipped at his face. He inched along the hood toward the nose of the truck. Soon Doobie had the Freightliner's nose just inches from the doors of the shiny Great Dane. Steadying himself with the taut end of the chain in his left hand, he used his right to wrap the other end of the chain about the latch handle of the stainless steel barn door. Then he pulled himself backward along the hood and braced himself against the windshield of the Freightliner.

He turned his head to look for a moment at Doobie, who sat wide-eyed, gripping the wheel fiercely with both hands. L.T. turned back to look at the trailer again, picked up the loose coils and tossed them forward as he nodded his head. Tires screeched and the Great Dane pulled away rapidly. It got so far away in the darkness that L.T. was thinking that the chain must have come loose and slipped off. Suddenly, the trailer door exploded with a bang and flew back toward him. He ducked and it sailed over his head clipping the roof of the tractor and bouncing onto the trailer. The heavy door dragged the steel links of the chain across L.T.'s arms, raking skin and flesh as he held his forearms in front of his face for protection. When the chain stopped he pulled on it to drag the door against the nose rack of the trailer. It jammed there, but gave him enough slack to reach the front of the tractor and maybe a foot beyond. He slid to the nose, held the chain taut and turned over on his belly. Slowly he slid his legs down the front grille of the tractor, feeling with his bare toes for the cutout step in the aluminum bumper. He was well beyond the point of no return when his toes finally locked in on the bumper and he stood straight up and looked again at Doobie.

Something caught the corner of his eye and he looked over his shoulder to see blue lights flashing in the southbound lane. Two FHP cars slowed and swung across the grassy median to take up the chase northbound. He wrapped one hand around the chain tightly. With the other he pointed his thumb over his shoulder at the Great Dane. The engine roared louder and he turned to watch the shiny trailer grow larger again. As they neared the trailer he caught sight of Cheryl curled up in fetal position and sitting with her back against stacks of waxed cartons of lettuce. Doobie moved the Freightliner in until it almost touched the trailer and L.T. grabbed the edge of the right door, let go the chain and hoisted himself in through the opening. He went to Cheryl and tried to rouse her. It was very cold in the trailer, but not freezing temperature he was sure. He checked her pulse. It was slow, but steady. He put Cheryl over his left shoulder and sat on the trailer floor, bare feet dangling over the edge, motioning for Doobie to move in close again. Blue lights flashed beside them as the first FHP car began to overtake the Great Dane. The Freightliner grew larger, Doobie inching the big rig closer and closer. L.T. had his right hand out, blood dripping from his arm, ready to grasp the chain. The trailer suddenly lurched sideways and his left side slammed into the edge of the right door of the Great Dane. Cheryl was slipping so he quickly leaned backward and hit the floor but managed to drag her limp body back up.

Blue lights illuminated clouds of dust in the median as the first police cruiser spun wildly out of control. The second approached but Doobie put his arm out the window and waved him back. The cruiser pulled up alongside the Freightliner and Doobie pointed at the rear of the trailer. L.T. had regrouped and was ready to try again. He perched on the edge of the trailer floor in the open doorway as Doobie again moved the giant rig closer. L.T. reached out and grasped the chain, slid over the edge of the trailer until his toes locked on to the bumper. He wrapped the chain about his arm to secure it, raised his buttocks off the trailer and stood erect on the front bumper of the silver Freightliner with his daughter slung over his shoulder and careened along I-75 at seventy miles per hour.

Doobie immediately began to feather the accelerator. As the Great Dane pulled away he flipped on the lights and studied his giant hood ornament in the orange glow of the roof markers. The truck bled off speed. By the time they rolled to a gentle stop, air brakes hissing aloud, L.T. was too cramped up to let go of the chain. He heard popping sounds and looked over his shoulder and up the road to watch the blue Kenworth and shiny Great Dane trailer fly past a row of police cars with lights flashing, then spin wildly out of control as it crossed the spike belt that flattened all tires. Its driver did a masterful job of getting it straightened out just in time to plow headlong into the side of a concrete bridge.

An EMS truck pulled up on the grassy shoulder next to the Freightliner. Two paramedics rushed to help Doobie lift Cheryl and L.T. off the nose of the diesel. The night became quiet and still as the diesel engine was finally shut down. No tires whined on the Interstate. All traffic in both directions had slowed to a crawl to view the carnage. The paramedics put Cheryl in the ambulance. One returned to tend to L.T.'s bloodied arms but he refused and told them to get her to the hospital. Before they closed the door, he climbed in with her and sat beside her. She wore an oxygen mask and the attendant was plugging an intravenous line into her arm but she managed to nod at L.T. He let out a long slow breath as they drove away.

Chapter Eighteen

Doobie showed up at the University of Florida Medical Center in Gainesville a few hours later to see how they were doing. L.T. was still barefoot but sporting numerous bandages about his extremities.

"She's going to be fine," he said to Doobie. "How can I thank you, man?"

"Drive me home. And maybe put in a good word for me with Ruby."

Natalie showed up at the hospital about midday and the two women talked L.T. into coming to Goodlettsville for a few days of healing. He knuckled under.

Marlin Sears was killed in the crash of his tractor-trailer as he attempted to outrun State Police trying to arrest him. In the wreckage of his trailer they found enough evidence, including two fingernails, which later proved to be those of murder victim Wade Burton, to close the case of the iceman. From the twisted steel heap that was a Kenworth tractor they took a nickel-plated revolver registered to the late Arnold Perkins, which was found to be the murder weapon in the Calvin Miles homicide. The FBI were satisfied that Perkins, Miles and iceman Ward Burton had been killed by Marlin "Fish" Sears. Gary Turner identified the tractor and trailer as his and retrieved his brother's memorial. The folks in Pasco County, including Sheriff Henry, were also convinced that Marlin Sears was the murderer of Arnold Perkins. Elvis Wood was subsequently released. When a search warrant was executed at Marlin Sears' ranch a newspaper clipping linked him to the death of a computer salesman near Marietta, Georgia. Further investigation revealed paint on the twisted front bumper of the Kenworth that was later matched to the BMW. That case was renamed a homicide but closed due to the death of the assailant.

L.T. phoned Ruby, who informed him that Chief Mackenzie had been arrested along with Orville Hennessey, Ned Dunphy, and Mayor Pruitt. The town was under the temporary protection of the Ohio State Police.

"It seems one senior OSP officer had recommended to town council that they strongly consider reinstating you and giving you the Chief's job," said Ruby. "They asked for your cell number. Should I give it to them?"

"Not yet," he said, and hung up.

Two days later the body of a man was discovered frozen stiff in a ditch near Auburn, Indiana.

Michael Day

About the Author

Michael Day was born and raised in the Southern Ontario agricultural community of Leamington, near the busiest truck border crossing in North America. A diesel mechanic by trade, he was soon lured onto the open road, spending several years hauling produce over the interstate system between Toronto and the Gulf States. Learning quickly that there is much more to driving a truck than just sitting behind the wheel, he has successfully combined wit and experience to weave a story that comes alive on the highways of America. Today he and wife Diane can be seen sailing their sloop 'Day by Day' on Lake Erie or cruising a Harley along the north shore.

Printed in the United States
837600001B

9 781410 703286